The Shocking "True" Story of Linky & Dinky

Page 1

Uncle Url's Middle-Aged Magic!

Page 135

Secret Web Sites

Page 199

by Mark N. Beeghly

"Uncle Url"

I'm taking care of business for Linky & Dinky & Binky

Linky & Dinky Enterprises
P.O. Box 418
Oldsmar, FL 34677

ISBN: 0-9768588-0-0

9 8 7 6 5 4 3 2 1

Cover design anonymous
"Linky & Dinky"©, "Uncle Url"©,
"Middle-Aged Magic"©, "Linky & Dinky's Secret Clubhouse"©
are registered trademarks of Linky & Dinky Enterprises

Printed and bound in the U.S.A.

Inquiries welcome from all press and
media organizations except Dr. Phil.

This book is lovingly dedicated to
Sherri, Caitlin and Cassidy,
who make every day wonderful.

And the cat, Oodaba Chait

The Shocking "True Story"
of Linky & Dinky

Linky and Dinky aren't particularly introspective, but sometimes they have curiosities which compel them to seek answers. Usually it's about ways of the world, like how can a finepoint magic marker be used to modify the UPC codes on stuff at the grocery store so it scans at a lower price? "Impossible!" I tell them, "The computer knows if it's accurate or not." Nevertheless, they try, and one time they *did* get a package of Oreos to ring up for $42.96. Defeat never stops them; they just keep trying, or veer off in favor of a new gambit. And typically whatever answer I provide serves only to spur them on to some other offbeat idea.

But I love them, I can't help it. The seemingly constant flow of ideas, projects, gags and wild pranks might tire some senior citizens, such as myself, but I find it keeps me feeling young, and I have to admit, invigorated. Oh sure, it's a bit unusual for an older unmarried gent to be guardian of a couple of brothers who should be fully capable of managing their own affairs. How old are Linky and Dinky anyway? Of course that's one of the questions I'm asked most often, but I can only answer the truth: the question doesn't apply to them any more. And that's the point of this story.

I sit to pen this tale the week our newsletter has surpassed 100,000 subscribers. That's quite a feat, and it's a most notable event for us, this June of the year 2000. *(Editor's note: as of publication, Linky & Dinky's newsletter has nearly 500,000 daily readers.)* We knew the big

number was coming, of course, but we didn't know the exact day. When it happened, it was late in the evening, and I was going over business in my office on the third floor of the house. I looked up from my desk, pulled off my visor, scratched my head then slapped the intercom button: "Come
in here, both of you. I've got some news!" Our entire compound, including the Secret Clubhouse, is wired with intercoms, speakers and cable modem hookups, so I knew they'd hear me wherever they were.

They didn't answer, which only mildly surprised me. It usually indicates they're involved with something dastardly, and three out of four times that means torment for Binky. Grimacing a bit, I punched Binky's channel on the intercom. "Binky? You there?" No answer, and I could hear my own voice through the speaker in Binky's room, since it's on the floor below mine. At this time of night, for Binky not to be in his room was ample evidence for me that something was afoot with the boys. For weeks I had planned special speeches for each of them, congratulating Linky & Dinky for surpassing the 100,000 subscriber milestone, and a rub of encouragement for Binky, although his popular Free Stuff newsletter was at least a year behind the boys. I hoped whatever ruckus was going on wouldn't dampen the drama of my prepared remarks, but I was sure it would.

So I stood and walked out to the top of the stairs to listen for a commotion, the way I've found is always best to locate them. Our house is an old wood frame three-story eclectic contraption, the foundation laid over 100 years ago. It's been built upon several times, and we're blessed with over two dozen rooms, although none of them are very large. The architect must have had a "labyrinth complex," because some of the rooms lead into adjacent rooms and then dead end, although other rooms have as many as four doors in them.

Years ago, as a child growing up in this house, I discovered that there is one particular path a visitor can take which would wind him through every room except the kitchen and two bathrooms. It's a perfect setup for a haunted house, and the wooden floors and walls, secret closets, crooked stairways between floors and twisted hallways frighten even me on dark stormy nights. The plumbing booms and rattles throughout the entire house, but I depend on those noises as a signal to confirm bath time is actually in progress. An exterior fire escape meanders from the third floor balcony to the second floor balcony to the ground, but I never use it. It's rickety, and I've ordered it only be used in the case of an actual fire.

As I descended the stairway to find everybody, I expected to hear their clatter immediately. I knew they had to be in the house, because I had personally locked up the Secret Clubhouse over an hour ago. The Clubhouse is built about 100 yards deep into our backyard. It's over 5,000 square feet by itself, not counting the parking lot for our visitors, but it still looks small in front of the miles of acreage which runs behind our property.

All the land behind the fence is owned by Uncle Sam, but it's never been used for anything that I can deduce. As far as the eye can see, the rolling waves of scrub brush with only a few trees has always been something of a mystery, but the Feds keep the "No Trespassing" signs current, replacing them about every 5 years.

We've jumped the fence and taken long illegal hikes inside the fence in the past, but we never found anything of interest - just a dirt road that, oddly, isn't overgrown with weeds. Somebody drives on it regularly, but I've never seen them, and the road is so long we've never come to the end. I suspect that my father, who originally built the main house, had good reason to root his family on this property, and I know he knew the purpose of the government land, but the secret died with him. We never found anything among his papers about it, but I still suspect one day we'll uncover the truth.

I heard a clang and a crash from the kitchen, and one of the boys crying "Stop it!" I quickly weaved around the old furniture, nearly slipping on the throw rug Aunt Purl made for us one year, and rounded the corner into the kitchen.

"I've been calling for you boys, what have you been..." and I saw it. A cake, at least that's what the plan had been, layered haphazardly over two feet high, like a crooked frosted pyramid. Apparently the spatula had been too slow going, and icing had been slopped on the sides by hand. The three boys were covered in the stuff, and Binky had a particularly amusing mustache of vanilla frosting. The pans and racks and egg shells and measuring cups and bowls and spoons and empty mix boxes (with wax paper bag inserts) littered the table in the center of the kitchen. The timer on the oven was still going "beep". A haze of dry powder hung in the air, covering most everything, especially Dinky's hair. Empty frosting cans, licked clean, had been piled high in a tower.

"We made a cake for the celebration!" Linky gushed, eyeing the door behind him should developing circumstances merit an escape plan. Linky was the higher IQ'd one, and he knew it, and if you ever met him you'd see a dollop of larceny twinkling in his eyes. He's quick, he's sharp, and he'll get Dinky or Binky in trouble with a well-placed suggestion or innocent call to action faster than I can blink my tired old eyes. He's not a bad bean, as beans go, but his fun-loving attitude can run a simple idea for a jolly good time into a major cleanup disaster. But he somehow stays above the fray and is never implicated alone for the mess - one or both of the other ones always seem to be involved, too.

I just gazed, my mouth open, at the monstrosity on the table, and then slowly I looked below the table to take in the hundreds and hundreds of candle boxes all over the floor. The colorful flat rectangles were everywhere, some crushed, some unopened, most with a yellow or pink or blue candle still protruding from the little cardboard flaps.

"We're putting a hundred thousand candles on the cake for the hundred thousand subscribers!" Dinky piped in, obviously delighted with himself and the idea. He continued to beam from ear to ear, expecting, I knew, a "Wow! Good idea!" to gush from my lips. I just stared at him, watching that Dinky-smile light up that Dinky-face, haloed by at least half a cup of cake mix in his hair. I let the ridiculous notion of 600 pounds of candles crushing 36 ounces of cake settle into my brain for a few moments, but finally I spoke.

"You can't put a hundred thousand candles on a cake!" I cried, exasperated. "They'll never fit! Where did you get all these candles?" My arms swept open around the room, still taking in the scene.

THE SHOCKING "TRUE" STORY OF LINKY & DINKY

The proud smile on Dinky's face never dimmed. "We're putting them on one at a time. It's fun!" he answered, never realizing for a second that three people would need to place over 33,000 candles each.

Thankfully most of the tiny boxes were still cased in several large cardboard containers that had "Acme Candle Company" printed on the side. My mind had already begun working on damage control. We'd still be able to ship most of them back.

"Binky got them for free," Linky offered. "Tell him, Binky."

I turned to face Binky, deliberately softening the look on my face. Binky was usually innocent of any wrongdoing, and he had never instigated a single mess in his whole life. He was the good kid, and I treated him as such. As much as I hold him up to Linky and Dinky as an example, it just never does any good.

"So Binky, please, do tell me, where did you get so many candles? And at no cost, you say?"

"Well," Binky stammered, directing his answer to the floor "I found them for free at this web site, you know, and they offered to send a free pack of ten candles to anybody if you just asked for them, you see, so I did the math, and I made this keyboard macro, you know, and I asked for them ten thousand times." Binky looked up, then turned his head down again, sensing that something was wrong with requesting a hundred thousand free candles, but not sure exactly what. The Acme Candle Company did send them, so

©Linky & Dinky Enterprises   www.linkydinky.com   Uncle-Url@linkydinky.com

6

it's difficult to find fault with Binky, but I'm sure their webmaster will soon be making changes to thwart attempts like this in the future.

I circled the cake and the boys, their eyes following me the whole time. I was finding it difficult to actually maintain a stance of anger, and evaluated the unopened candle boxes and the thousands already scattered about in piles.

"Let's clean this up," I said, "and put all the candles we can back into their little boxes, and then we're going to ship as many as we can back to the company. I can't believe they would actually send you a hundred thousand birthday candles, but we're sending them back." I watched their spirits sink as I looked at each boy in turn. "GET BUSY!" I barked.

The three of them jumped because I raised my voice, which I seldom do, but promptly sat on the floor, pushing the little candles back into the little boxes as fast as their frosted fingers would let them.

"Linky, you do the dishes. Clean up the table and all the mess."

"And when all of it's done, we'll eat the cake, because we hit the magic number tonight." I turned to leave, with my face pointed away so they couldn't see the giant smile on my face. There was no sense in diminishing the strength of my authoritative commands.

Cheers started flying around the room at the news, and Linky and Dinky performed their oft-practiced High Five routine, spinning and going low, going high, on the side, the whole bit.

   "Hurry up!" I said, walking out of the room. "And bring some cake slices up to my office when you're finished, so we can celebrate in proper fashion."

   What I didn't know as I left the room was that the gathering about to take place in my office between the three boys and myself was the last time we would all be together.

CHAPTER TWO

I waited in my office for over an hour as the boys cleaned up the multiple messes in the kitchen. They knew my personal level of expectation for cleanliness and attention to detail, and of course they would clean no more thoroughly than that. I didn't expect polished counters and cabinets, nor did I expect freshly waxed floors, but I did assume the clutter would be picked up and the muck wiped clean.

I sat at my desk waiting, reading over the notes I'd made to mark this most festive occasion of attaining 100,000 subscribers to our weekly newsletter. It might seem corny to some, to make a speech to Linky and Dinky and Binky about progress, about where we've been and where we were going, but I thought I had a few clever lines so, by golly, I was going to deliver it. I had already written and printed the cover letter to the Acme Candle Company, and I would give that to Binky to send to the company with the remainder of the 100,000 candles, although I'm afraid the boys had already used a thousand or more of the candles. The profuse apologies within the letter would hopefully spare us any expense -- I was gambling that the company would just be thrilled to have the bulk of them back in saleable condition.

I decided to tidy up my office to set a good example. Most of the furniture in my office I inherited from my father, Ramford Url, including the oversized roll top desk which was his pride and joy, and is now, in turn, my most prized piece. It's an authentic Cutler, and was top-of-the-line in 1900. I still have the original keys for the 10-pin lock, the special inset locking bars directly incorporated into the ends and center of the roll top cover. The desk is a beaut, and I've kept the deep-rubbed mahogany gleaming with a special polish at least twice a year. This particular model has two hidden cubbies and a special foot rest that pops out near the floor with the swing of an iron lever. I drilled tiny holes in the back flanking, a standard practice today to allow wires for telephones and lamps and computers, but of course those holes weren't necessary in 1900. It hurt me to take a power tool to the majestic desk, but I just kept telling myself it was an upgrade. I wasn't about to sell it, although I'm sure it would fetch five figures, so drilling the holes didn't hurt the value of the piece, and in fact it made it more valuable to me by way of adding usefulness. That's what I convinced myself, anyway.

The rest of the office was standard for an old house. Three of four walls were built-in bookshelves, but I had as many knickknacks and mementos on the shelves as I did books. Two older sofas had migrated up here a few decades ago as the living room received new ones, and a few occasional chairs and small tables were appro-priately positioned around the egg-shaped rug in the center (another gift from Aunt Purl. Without her, the house would surely resemble a bachelor pad. She didn't live with us, but she kept our house looking more like a home and less like a locker room than I could alone. Aunt Purl was my sister, of course, the name "Purl" a take off on our family name, "Url" (the little ones found "Aunt Url" hard to say, and it always seemed to come out "Purl" instead). Although neither her nor I were actually blood relations to Linky or

Dinky, we were still family. I'll get to that later, it's actually the whole point of this story.)

The clamor of the three boys coming up the stairs signaled it was time. Linky carried several slices of cake on an old turkey platter, leading the others as he always does, while Binky sported a fistful of forks in one hand and a tenuously balanced stack of small plates in the other. Dinky trailed the others carrying a glass jug of punch and a short stack of paper cups.

"Uncle Url -- who, exactly, was the hundred thousandth subscriber?" Linky asked, assembling the goodies and tools in the space I'd cleared on one of the tables.

"I'll have to look back," I answered, glancing at the computer display on my desk. "It happened over an hour ago and we've gotten dozens more subscribers since then. Why do you ask?"

"We should give them a free Clubhouse membership!" Dinky said excitedly, plopping himself down on one of the couches, plate of cake on his lap and fork in hand.

"I want to put their picture at the entrance of the Clubhouse with a plaque underneath saying they were the hundred thousandth. That would be cool!" Linky explained.

I took my own plate of cake and settled into the high-backed chair at my desk. I took a bite before responding.

"I supposed we could do that, but I don't know if he'd want to have his picture in the Clubhouse." I took another bite and continued, "But he might, and maybe we could set up a backdrop of flowers and balloons and such, with a big sign reading 'Linky & Dinky's 100,000th Subscriber!' and take his picture in front of it, like a real award."

Binky immediately spoke "I saw one of those big arches of tissue flowers behind the high school near the dumpsters! They had it for the Prom, for the king and queen to stand in front of. It's been there for weeks, and it would be perfect! We could bring it over here and put up our own sign - I'll make the sign, it won't cost us a thing!"

I had to smile, and I nearly choked as I wondered what Binky was doing near the dumpsters behind the high school, but I decided to let that pass. "Are they throwing it away?" I asked. Binky nodded, his mouth full again. "Well, I think I'd better call the office at the high school and ask them if we may borrow it, before we just take it." I finished the thought on paper, making a note to call the school's administration office the next day. "Also, I'll shoot an e-mail to the winner, too, to explain what happened and ask them if they want to participate for a free Clubhouse membership."

We finished our cake in silence, then I commenced to give my speeches. The boys sat quietly, only two-thirds attentive, and mostly agreed with what I had to say. I won't bother you with the text of my prepared remarks, but suffice it to say it fit the bill of an old guy trying to pep talk young people who largely didn't understand, or care, for that matter. By the end, Dinky was rolling on the floor - not laughing or anything, just rolling around. It's his way. Binky combined all the crumbs of all remaining cake from all the plates into one pile and attempted to shape it back into a proper slice. Frugality, it seems, often makes for odd compulsions.

All of a sudden Linky shouted "Dinky is tearing up your desk!"

We all jumped, including Dinky, who apparently had been laying prone next to the desk, fingering some portion near the floor.

"Dinky! What are you doing?" I demanded.

"Nothing!" was Dinky's retort, but his hand was suspiciously near the foot of my prized Cutler Rolltop desk.

I bent down to study the area where Dinky had been active, looking for damage. "What exactly were you doing?" I asked in a softer voice. I noticed something unusual about the wood in that area.

"I was just pulling at this piece of wood," Dinky answered. "It was loose and I was trying to push it back in."

"Loose? What's loose? Nothing should be loose down there," I said more to myself than to anyone else. I peered closer, now down on my knees, as I examined the finger of mahogany Dinky pointed out.

I slid it up and down, and was surprised to find it moved easily. The thin band of mahogany, almost invisible when placed in exactly the right position, was sculpted and slotted in a deliberate design. It appeared to belong there, and it also appeared to be removable.

So I removed it. It slid out and I held it in my hand. About 3 inches long, carefully slotted and sanded, it had been holding something in place, like a sliding latch.

Without even taking the time to think, I reached back to the area where the sliver of wood had been, inserted my fingers into the trough and pulled a bit. Without so much as a "how do you do?" the entire side panel of my stoic roll top opened outward, hinged by I know not what.

Pressed into a cavity, now revealed by the open door, an old book, like a ledger, leather-covered and embossed with a series of numbers, stood waiting. I stared at it, hardly noticing how the boys had gathered around my crouched body, and we all just looked at the book, hushed by the surprise of it all.

"It's a book!" Linky commented.

"Guh duh," Dinky mocked. "It's mine! I found it!" and he reached up to grab it.

I knocked Dinky's hand away immediately. This desk was over 100 years old, and had been in the possession of my father for the first 60 years, and myself for the last 40 years. Whatever this book was, it most certainly wasn't Dinky's.

Very slowly, I pulled the book loose and took it in my hands. It was old, no doubt about that, and the numbers on the cover were embossed in gold, much like an old King James Bible. It took only a few seconds, and I realized what they were: longitude and latitude.

"That's strange," I said to the boys, pointing at the title of the book. "This looks like a longitude and latitude position. I wonder where? And why, for that matter."

Linky was on the case. He jumped across the room, grabbed the base of my standing globe and dragged it over. I called out the numbers to him, and he found it almost immediately.

"It's here." Linky announced. "It's right on our town, so maybe it's our yard or somewhere nearby!"

Thoughts of buried treasure or secret catacombs flooded my imagination. We'd need a GPS system to find the exact spot. I was just reading in a Sunday paper advertising insert about them, and how you can punch in a location and it will guide you to it. But that would be for later. I stood with the book and returned to my chair in front of the desk. Dinky continued to peer around the secret compartment in my desk, and I let him, for I didn't see how anything else could still be inside.

Binky stood over my shoulder, with Linky on my left side as I opened the front cover. The very first thing I noticed was my father's signature, at the bottom of the first page in his distinctive flourish. So my father had owned this book, I thought to myself, and probably had written it, but never told anyone he had hid it - or why. More questions excited my brain and I read the first page aloud:

"This book, my legacy, contains the knowledge I obtained while researching the beast. I do not claim it to be complete, only that it is as

much as I have uncovered during my short years on this earth.
My work continues, and I expect this journal to survive me, unfinished. I have documented the beginnings, the growth and the current stages of the beast as I know them to be, true and honest, and my educated assumptions about the future path the beast will take, and the final incarnation it will form. I offer no other answers other than those contained herein, and on the cover."

Respectfully submitted,Ramford Url, August, 1917

I looked to Linky, saying nothing more, as if he could make sense of this. He looked back at me, his mind whirling behind his eyes, but said nothing.

Through simple happenstance, everything had suddenly changed. The discovery of the hidden compartment, the book with a title pinpointing the position of the Linky & Dinky compound on the planet, and the inexplicable writings of my father over 80 years ago. A beast? For God's sake, what was he talking about? I knew my father as well as any man could. He worked at the university, often out of town on research projects, but when at home he played with me upon his knee, taught me of driving cars and honesty (and a little about girls), why the grass was green, how to throw a fast ball, vacations, and all the usual stuff. I thought nothing special of him, other than he was my very own father, and all the personal feelings that that entails.

The book shocked us all, and it meant more surprises, contained within as surely as its hiding for 80 years had a purpose.

And why the embossed longitude and latitude of our town? What could be at that exact spot? We had to find out. It must have been very important. But that project would have to wait until daylight tomorrow. My father's heavy book would certainly give a clue, and I was ready to find out whatever it had to say.

"Okay boys, get comfortable. I'm about to turn the page..."

CHAPTER THREE

My father's journal felt heavy in my hands. The opened first page describing the contents -- he called it his "legacy" -- sent my memories racing back forty, and then fifty years, as close to the time the book was being written as I could possibly recall.

Ramford Url would spend long hours in his office, and although I've claimed the old corner room on the third floor as my office for over 40 years, it's still his. I still feel like I'm just using it in his absence. Long before the internet, before television, even before the first World War, my father diligently applied his powerful intellect to the pursuits of research in this room, at this desk, the specifics of which I never really knew what. Now I wish I had paid more attention. He gave talks at the university, I remember that, and he held some kind of position of high regard. If I dug up his old certificates and awards I'd find out exactly what they were, but Aunt Purl took a lot of my father's old things when he died (the wisdom being that she'd be a better caretaker of his history than I.) Aunt Purl actually might have a much better idea about this mysterious book than I do, and she'll be the first telephone call I make come the morning. As my sister, she always grasped angles of what was going on that I never could, or at least never did.

Biology was a big thing with my father, and he held several degrees in the sciences of life. He'd be amazed at that discipline today -- common knowledge of biology in the year 2000 is leaps and bounds beyond what was known in his day. My father died without ever knowing about DNA! He was at the forefront of evolutionary sciences at the early part of the century, though that ilk of researchers kept quietly to themselves, never wishing to stir up the anger of the faith-based public activists, which heavily outnumbered them. A few brave (meaning "young") Naturalists of the day would publish something outrageous about Evolution and get his heathen butt royally kicked, but mostly they studied in the dead of night, writing and experimenting.

Linky sat back on the nearest of the old sofas, pen and scratch paper already in hand, prepared to jot down anything clueful that might pop up. Dinky and Binky sat cross-legged on the floor, watching me with anticipation, as if I was about to tell a scary campfire story. The setting was certainly perfect for it; night was well underway, and the unshaded window above my roll top desk framed a magnificent full moon, swept with dark wispy clouds.I took a deep breath, turned the page, and studied it for a moment. My father's heavy handwriting would be a bit difficult to wade through, but I was sure I could do it. Certain areas of the paper were washed out, probably from nothing but age, and a couple of dark brown spots on the edges betrayed a coffee spill, wiped off and forgotten decades ago.

I pushed my bifocals flush to my face, and began to read aloud:

Some eighty thousand years before the birth of Christ, in what would be known by those in the distant future as the Northwestern Utah Salt Flats, a loosely organized community of pre-civilized human beasts thrived amidst what was then a jungle terrain.

These early humans, still animals, ate of the vibrant vegetation; they used clubs and sharpened sticks to slay small wildlife. They devised a way to cook the carcasses in a festive daily ritual over crude rotisseries fashioned from stacked stones and stripped tree limbs. The often uncontrolled fires would sear the fur, the skin and the meat together into a mass of burnt animal, yet the aroma aroused their hunger. Ripping the encrusted surfaces away with their uncorrected teeth, the new humans ingested the raw, the cooked and the scorched meat together, without discernment, and nourishment was had. They didn't know the word "delicious", but the bloody leg shank raised over the head and the beaming smile told the others the day's food was good.

Each day of the tribe comprised hours of endless hunting. Each afternoon saw vicious and bitter infighting among the men over shelter and food and the females, while during the fire-lit evenings ignorant children watched each chase and loud spat end in public copulation. Sleep came only after it overpowered fear of the night.

On one of these nights, beyond the shrinking circle of light cast by the tribe's dying fire, the first stirrings are quietly made in the newest incarnation of a very old life form.

And it's a beast, too.

"A beast!" Dinky yelled, flailing his hands in the air, "I knew this would be a COOL story!" "You entirely missed the part about 'public copulation'," Binky stated, as a taunt, "It went right over your pointy little head."Linky leaned forward, already a thinking ahead of the other boys, and probably ahead of me to, with an understanding of where this journal's tale might head. "How did Grampa Url know about the cavemen?" Linky asked me. "I guess he knew what all the other historians and scientists knew," I started to answer, "but none of them were actually around during the caveman days. They can figure out what it was like by digging up bones and pottery and stuff." I paused a bit, and realizing my own ignorance, I finished: "Heck, I have no idea, Linky. No idea at all."

"Can we burn some meat like that and feed it to Binky?" Dinky asked, pointing at his frugal cousin, who in turn made no secret he was revolted by the thought."Pipe down, everybody. Let me continue." I ordered. "We'll never figure this out until we get to it."

I shuffled about in my chair, and continued to read to the boys:

Warm winds stirred up by the rising sun swept through the tribal clearing, but the last warm embers of the fire failed to flame back to life.

The circle of sleeping primitive humans were startled from slumber by the guttural cry of one of the females as she realized her newest baby was missing. The tiny ones usually cried for mother's milk continuously, but the baby was taken early in the night, and without his grumbling complaints, the female had slept soundly, blissfully unaware of her instinctual duties.

The primitive mom crawled around her bed of dead leaves, brushing aside the deeper layers of brush in a vain search for her seven pound manchild. Unable to understand the ways of the world around her, she continued to cry out, and quickly came to realize her baby was gone for good. The instinct of motherhood raged strong within her, and her wail grew louder and forlorn. One of the men, perhaps the baby's father, annoyed at the loud noise so soon after awakening, walked over and pushed her down, a roar and violent shaking of his head making clear the meaning he didn't like the noise. He didn't know how to say "quiet!", and she didn't know how to tell him the child was gone, but she deduced his desire for silence, even though he didn't understand her loss.

A short distance away, but well within the sound of the mother's suddenly snuffed cry, a wild boar dined on the morsels of what the stealthy jungle dog had stolen. How many humans had been meals for the wild dogs? Countless. How many wild dogs had been meals for the humans? Again, countless, but Nature makes no rules for conduct, and she does not impose ethics. Food is food. After the boar loses interest, but before the sun sets this day, insects will swarm over the remains until no soft tissue remains at all. Over the ensuing months, simple bacteria and common oxygen will chew on the thin spindly bones until they vanish. Food is food.

Only vaguely aware a child is missing, and even that soon to be forgotten during the day's hunt, the men leave the women and other children behind and crunch through the underbrush toward what they don't have the language to call "the hunting place". And so another cycle begins on the planet they didn't know would be called Earth, and the gigantic global chaos of life continues in wobbly balance, singing in rough harmony and slowly, very slowly, all around the world, new tricks are learned by accident, are remembered, are shared, and the sluggish march toward civilization continues. Man would one day conquer the earth and all it contains, but not without first conquering language.

Language was the last thing on the minds of these primitive humans.

But the new beast in the jungle had language. The new beast, very old in time yet new to the Earth, understood all the movements of all the life around it. And it knew language; all languages. The words of life and death and food and fight and children and shelter. It knew the symphony of photosynthesis and the circle of evaporation and the mathematical power of growth by cell division. It knew well the intricate plans devised by the language of DNA; it knew of chemical reactions and electricity and all about the gigantic reptilian creatures who once owned the earth. It knew of gravity, of magnetic fields, of weather, and of the massive waves of photons streaming from the sun providing illumination. From the growth of crystals to the process of digestion, the new beast in the jungle was well versed. It had learned it all and lived it all before on a millions of worlds in thousands of galaxies over immeasurable time. Life was the same everywhere.

Everything was the same everywhere. And it would be the same here.

I let the heavy book rest back on my knee, and I looked up at the boys. The mood in the room had most definitely changed, and not for the better. "How did Grampa Url know about DNA?" Linky asked. "DNA wasn't discovered until after he died..." his voice trailed off at that.We all sat in silence, pondering what we had just learned from my Father's journal, until Dinky broke the silence.

"Uncle Url?" Dinky whispered. I looked over to Dinky and met his eye. "I'm scared." he said. I continued to look at Dinky, not sure how to respond, until I finally acknowledged that he was right to be scared. "Me too, Dinky," I answered him. "Me too."

CHAPTER FOUR

This situation was scary, and I had no idea how worse it might get. My father had knowledge of DNA in 1917? A highly detailed story of primitive culture and a "beast" which came from other worlds and knew everything about Earth and humans and how we work? It was not only scary, it was impossibly bizarre, and I would have to pull this stuff closer to the vest. It may not be good for the boys to be aware of the rest of it. They would probably already be having nightmares tonight. My father must have had a reason for keeping this information secret and shielded from the rest of us, and I should probably do the same. At least until I found out if it was a joke from the grave or actually a revelation about our unknown history.

"Okay, all of you go to bed." I ordered. The expected noises, wails, howls and moans came right on cue. "Why can't we hear more of the story!" Linky begged, his face screwing up in a frown. Similar requests rang in from Dinky and Binky as well. "Because it's too much to read, too late to read it, and I'm not sure this book is intended for anybody other than myself." I offered, trying to sound definite and sure. But I expected more argument as I rose from my chair and pointed toward the door. "Bed. Now. All of you." "Okay!" Linky yelled, running for the door. Something not right about that, but I let him go. Dinky and Binky left too, but not so enthusiastically.

With the first part of "getting the boys to bed" underway, I would wait a little while before making the rounds to finish the chore. I carried the heavy leather-covered book to one of the sofas and plopped myself down on one side, near the light. I ran my fingers over the embossed title, a longitude and latitude numerical code for a position on the globe. Why would my father title a book in such a way? I couldn't fathom it, nor the reason for taking the trouble to have the numbers embossed in gold leaf, like a Bible. My head continued to swim with conflicting ideas, trying, and failing, to make it all fit together in one calm, sensible bundle. Nothing about any of it was calm or sensible.

I flipped to the last page I had read, and continued reading, this time to myself. I made a mental note to mark this spot in my memory, so as to not discuss any of the new details with the boys.

The unthinkable horror of a baby stolen in the night to become food for the wildlife meant nothing to the Beast, and not that much more to the primitive mother as the daily toils of collecting unnamed fruits and berries occupied all her attention. By nightfall she remembered the infant only because her breasts hurt from the swell of untapped milk. She squeezed them to reduce the pressure, and lapped up the dribble with a filthy finger. Other infants suckled from other females, but helping feed the other babies did not occur to her.

Only a short distance away from the primitives, the Beast lay in the jungle as a boulder, as a giant rock covered over with moss and fallen leaves and trees and weeds that found a way to poke up to the sunlight through the heavy cover of forest vines. The Beast was part of the earth, two thirds buried in the soil, resting in the same spot it hit the day it fell from the sky...

Linky burst into my office shouting "Uncle Url! I found the exact spot the cover of the book is talking about, it's here! It's our house!" he rushed in, and kept talking "I went to a web site where you enter longitude and latitude, and it brings up a map of the exact spot with roads and everything just like a real map! Come look! It's on my computer! It's our house!"

I laid the book on the sofa beside me, placing a bookmark in the page (something Binky had received by the dozen for free from a web site) and stood up. "Okay, okay, show me." and I followed him as he zoomed out of the room, heading, I knew, to the computer in his bedroom. Linky ran far ahead of me, and I followed, lumbering down the hardwood floor of the hallway at a respectable rate, and I took the steps down to the second floor at double time, but after I rounded the corner toward Linky's room, I stuck my head into Dinky's bedroom as I passed and commanded: "Lights out!". I saw Dinky jump, startled, but I kept walking, assuming it would take a bit more to actually bolt him down for the night.

Linky's room was disheveled, as usual. Dozen of boxes were strewn about, almost all software packages, some with books and flyers and inserts protruding from the half-closed flaps. They were all over the room, stacked along the walls in no apparent order. His collection of promotional items also littered the flat surfaces on the furniture around the room; mouse pads, magnetic stickers and lapel pins (some with tiny flashing strobe lights) were stuck to various horizontal and vertical surfaces, hawking assorted corporate logos. Linky's AOL Christmas Tree hung from the ceiling fan, built entirely from the flood of AOL software CDs which hit his snailmailbox regularly (and from magazines and loaves of bread and every software package ever shipped.) It was a beautiful thing, and twinkled and wobbled when the ceiling fan was running, a testament to AOL's marketing machine.

I stepped up to Linky's computer which dominated his desk. His sleek Macintosh G4 with gobs of memory has more horsepower than I understand how to describe. He has the best computer in the house, which shouldn't surprise anyone, and he really knows how to use it (as the song goes). Linky was patiently pointing to a spot on his monitor, and I bent down to study it, lifting my nose to be able to see through my bifocals. A star marked the spot, and I noticed the road names directly around our house. Yep. The longitude and latitude embossed on the cover of my father's journal was without a doubt pinpointed to our house.

"So now what?" I asked, recovering from the crouch over to the computer. A little crick in my back flared momentarily, and I swung a hand around to comfort it. "What does it mean?" "It means the journal can be found here." Linky answered, but not so sure himself. "But that doesn't really make sense -- why hide a book with the instructions to find it on the hidden book itself? Dumb."

"If we move the book across the street, will the title of it change?" Dinky asked, having entered the room without our noticing. He sat on the floor cross-legged, intending to stay awhile. "No, of course not," I answered, while Linky muttered "dork" at the same time. "But I've got another idea." I continued. "What if the point of the journal that Grampa Url wrote is the location?" I looked at both boys, waiting for that to sink in. After a few more seconds I went on, "What if he built this house, on this spot, because of what he had discovered and wrote about in the journal?"

A low-toned "ohhhh..." emanated from Linky, and he turned to look at Dinky, who said "Huh?" "It's genius!" Linky called out, "By using the longitude and latitude on the cover of the book, and probably other places inside, it wouldn't matter where the book ended up or in what time or what language, the finders could always track it back to this location."

Linky's face was lit up like a nighttime football game. "It must have been very important to Grampa Url that the book and this house be kept together!" "So we've got to find the buried treasure!" Dinky shouted. "Let's go dig up the cellar!" "Oh no you don't, you're not digging up anything." I ordered. "Nobody is going into that cellar but me. It's far too old and dangerous." I turned to leave the room, knowing I had several hours of reading still ahead of me this night. "And right now, you are both going to BED!" So I headed back to my office, calling a Good Night to Binky as I passed his room (Binky could always be counted on to behave).I was sorely tempted to telephone Aunt Purl, but I knew she was long ago retired for the night, and waking her now, with this news, would only keep her up and chattering until daybreak. Calling her in the morning would be better.

After a few minutes, the house grew still and quiet, and the boys were finally down for the night. I continued to read my father's journal, growing more confused, and I must admit, a bit fearful at where this was leading. The tension did not stop growing as I turned each page.

From under the skull of the dead human baby a Beast tentacle arose from the ground. Transparent as water, the Beast stretched a gelatinous finger up through the bloody dirt and searched the surface of the cranium for an opening. Finding what had been the break in the skull for the left ear, the tentacle pushed into the brain mass and immediately began branching out. Dozens of slithers plied through the gray matter, absorbing it whole, and the Beast understood it, finding it quite similar to the other bipeds scattered in groups across the world, with only minor differences.

They slept again, these primitives, and the night called noisily like any other night, threatening danger, but the humans felt safe within the glow of the fire.

From under the soil, tentacles reached upward toward the sleeping bodies, gripping on the skin it could find, roaming over their bodies in search of cavities. When a suitable opening was found, the tips of the tentacles broke off, remaining inside their respective human, continuing a journey inside the bodies to the brain. Before the Beast's tentacles has receded back into the ground, the parasitic tips had already located their respective intelligence cores and settled in for the lifespans of these humans. It was to be an interesting ride.

The next morning found the primitives talking, each possessing a common vocabulary of several thousand words. They thought nothing of how this came to be, but found speech and communication a new and wonderful toy. They suddenly had names for everyday items, like trees and sky and berries and fruits. The urge to make new words was strong, and they named each other before the day was out, and for once the women could tell the men what they did all day, and the men regaled the women with tales of hunting glory. Laughter became a part of their day, and ideas began to be shared about new ways to make shelter, and ways to trick the prey into traps, and a sense of community grew where there had only been uneasy competitors before. And so they started their own little civilization, the Beast guiding the way.

But the Beast wasn't anywhere near finished with this species yet. After a time, after much more time, the Beast would make a move again.

I couldn't take anymore, so I quickly marked the page and tossed the book beside me on the couch. All of a sudden I had recalled something my father had said to me many decades ago, but after having been long forgotten, I remembered it now clearly and plainly. I had misunderstood it, in fact, ignored what he told me back then, but now I knew it must be crucially important to the story in his journal. My father, Ramford Url, the scientist, had told me: "Not only are things not as they seem, they didn't happen the way we were told, and in fact, they aren't happening at all."

It was a clue that served only to deepen the mystery. And I knew in my bones it involved Linky and Dinky and Binky. But How? I couldn't fathom.

CHAPTER FIVE

Thankfully, I don't remember my dreams that night. I had read my father's mysterious journal for another hour or so until I simply could not keep my eyes open any longer. I did awake for a moment, after a loud Bang emitted from somewhere near Dinky's room, but I ignored it. Dinky often flipped over in the night and slammed his foot or hand into the wall. It never bothered him, so I never investigated.

Morning came (for me) when Linky pounded on my closed bedroom door and shouted at the top of his voice: "Uncle Url! Wake Up! I Found Out Something!" The pounding on the door continued.

So I arose, checked my nightshirt and opened the door for Linky. "What is it?" I asked, perturbed.

"It's directly in the center of our house." Linky blurted out, breathless. "I plotted the exact location of the longitude and latitude and it's precisely the middle of our house. And that's the middle of the living room, so it has to mean the cellar or the attic!" he finished.

"Okay, okay," I answered, sitting back down on the bed, still confused. "Wait a minute. Last night you already figured out the location was our house, why are you shouting about it now?"

"Because I found another web site that can zoom in closer on the longitude and latitude, and I plotted the spot to be exactly in the exact center of our house!" Linky explained. There was no slowing him down. "So we have to go into the cellar and see what's there!"

I ruminated on that news for a few seconds, and stood back up. "Alright, okay, let me get dressed and I'll go have a look. What are Binky and Dinky doing?" I asked. "They're both still in bed." "Well leave them be. I don't need a circus going on down there." I walked toward my bathroom, "Give me a few minutes and I'll be down-stairs." "Okay!" Linky gushed, and scooted out the door and thundered down the stairs to wait.

I went about an abbreviated version of my morning constitutional, taking special care not to use the hot water tap on the sink, knowing that to use it would make the pipes erupt into a loud, guttural wail which might wake the other boys. Let sleeping Dinkys lie, I always say.

Linky was in the living room, standing at the old door which led to the cellar. The door was old and scratched from countless bangs and bashes the boys inflicted upon it and other vertical surfaces as they had run around like wild banshees over the years. Not so much now, but when they were younger, no shiny surface had been immune or protected from marring. The door leading to the cellar was underneath the main staircase which led to the second and third floors, and hadn't been opened in over 10 years. I kept the key hidden in my dresser, and I now held it in my hand ready to open the lock.

"Linky, nobody has been down there in a decade, and it was dank and wet and noisy with God-knows-what back then. I do not want you to come down until I check it out." I lectured.

"I understand," Linky answered, and handed me the flashlight he had been holding.

"Thanks," I said, and stuck the key in the lock. It turned easily, and the door swung open without a sound. I reached in and switched on the light -- nothing. Bulb burnt out or the switch was rusted. I wasn't surprised, and flicked on the flashlight and stepped inside.

As I slowly moved down the stairs, checking each step before I put full weight upon it, the dusty moist atmosphere struck me full strength. It was still breathable, but just.

At the bottom, the dirt floor was a bit mushy, and I splayed the light around my feet to check it out for safety. I could have stepped into a rat's nest and not have been the least bit surprised. A faint light from daybreak was seeping in through the tiny windows near the ceiling, which were actually at ground level outside the house. The muck which covered the glass substantially reduced the lighting, and also made it impossible to peer into the darkness from the outside. The heavy overgrown bushes which ringed our home also reduced the sun's attempt to break through.

Standing still, I swung the beam around the room. I remembered most of what I saw, and could identify it: old crates filled with junk, a long forgotten stack of lumber from some building project, a tall mound of firewood we'd never used, a rusted dinette which I recalled used to be on the back porch, and lots of little pools of water. Were it to be measured by the square foot, over three fourths of the cellar was empty. I lifted the light to the ceiling, finding heavily dusty rafters and a few pipes running across and disappearing up into the main house.

Nothing was here.

I turned around to call up for Linky to come down, but I caught his eye instead. He had been peering down the steps watching me the whole time. "Can I come down now?" Linky asked.

"Yeah, come on. Go slowly on those steps!" I warned. Linky almost instantly appeared at my side, and pointed to the right. "That's the center, right where that column is."

I moved the flashlight toward that direction and saw the column: it was wide, probably 8 inches in diameter, made of what looked like a telephone pole. A bit of moss (or something dark greenish, anyway) grew on it in patches. We both tiptoed over to get a closer look, mindful of the puddles of water surrounding it. "So you think this is the exact center of the house?" I asked quietly.

"Yes, look around. It's in the exact center of the cellar, and the cellar is the same size as the house." Linky answered. "This is load bearing," I commented. "The weight of the floor above is resting on it. This is a very important piece of the house." I rapped the column with my knuckles in several different places, not really sure what I was looking for, but it seemed like an appropriate thing to do. Linky started knocking as well. The sounds our tapping made were all the same. Nothing hollow about this staff of wood.

"There's nothing here, Linky. How sure are you of the location? Longitude and latitude isn't so close even when the seconds are used."

"The web site I used said it pinpointed the spot to within a 12 foot diameter, and that circle is directly over our house." Linky explained. "Maybe Grampa Url just meant to identify our house, or this land, but not necessarily an exact spot inside the house. He would have included more instructions were that the case." I was trying to convince myself as well as Linky. I knew more about the contents of the book than Linky did, and with that in mind, I knew something larger than a hidden spot in the house was at hand.

Linky wasn't ready to give up. His hand had been resting flat against the pole while I was talking, and his eyes suddenly lit up: "Feel this, Uncle Url!" he said excitedly. "Put your hand on this, it's vibrating!"

I did, and indeed I could feel a vibration. We both moved our flattened palms around the pole and a steady humming vibration could be felt.

"Well, that's really not surprising," I ventured, "the whole house is resting on it, surely that accounts for the vibration." But Linky had already moved across the cellar to another column and was hugging it.

"Nope! This one is not vibrating!" he exclaimed. He ran to another pole and felt it too. "Not this one, either!"

I felt foolish standing in the dark in the cellar holding a telephone pole tightly in my hands, so I announced: "Alright, we have a vibrating weight-bearing pole in our cellar at the exact spot my father pinpointed on the cover of a journal he wrote over 80 years ago." I chuckled to myself. "Not really much to get excited about, Linky."

"What's vibrating?" Dinky asked, jumping down the final step to the cellar. "I want to feel it!"

"Me too!" Binky added, following Dinky across the cellar, jumping over the pools of water Dinky sloshed through.

A party in the cellar was the last thing I wanted, so I got gruff: "Alright, feel this and we're all going back upstairs." I moved aside and let Dinky and Binky touch the pole for a few seconds. "That's enough, let's go!" I commanded, and motioned the boys toward the steps.

I followed them all up, reminding Dinky to go changes his socks and shoes because they were wet now with stagnant water from the cellar. I quickly shut the cellar door, re-locked it, and pocketed the key.

The rest of the morning vanished after I got Aunt Purl on the phone. We talked for hours about the puzzling book and the crazy things it implied. I read portions of the journal to her, including the part about the primitives suddenly learning language from some rock-thing in the jungle. After that, she was silent, and then I could tell she was gently sobbing.

"Purl, what is it?" I asked softly. She continued to weep, but was trying to recover herself. I waited patiently.

"It's just something... something I just remembered," she finally said in a weak voice. "Something about all this that I think means something," she finished.

"Yes? What?" I asked, and continued to wait a few seconds, and then asked again. "What is it, Purl? What do you remember?"

"Grampa Url, he, uh..." she stopped again. I waited. I knew she wanted to tell me, it was just a matter of waiting for her to fully collect herself.

"Grampa Url," she started again, "he built this house... oh my... oh my dear..." she trailed off. The suspense was killing me.

"Yes, he built this house over 100 years ago. I know that, we all know that. What are you saying?" I tried hard to not sound exasperated.

"Well, I don't remember what we were talking about at the time, because I was very little, but for some reason I asked him why we lived here. You know, a child's question about why we live in a certain house in a certain spot in a certain town, you know."

"Yes, go on." I prodded.

"When I asked him that, why do we live in this house or some-thing like that, I remember what he answered." She paused again. I said nothing. "I remember exactly what he said."

I could hear Aunt Purl drawing a breath, then she finally spoke: "He said 'Can you think of a better way to hide something than to build a house over it?'"

I sucked in a gasp of air and held it a long time. When I finally released it, the words came tumbling out:

"Purl," I exclaimed, "he built the house on top of that rock thing."

"I know," she whimpered, "I know."

CHAPTER SIX

All during my phone conversation with Aunt Purl, activity in our house ran its course as usual, although I tuned it out as the intensity of our talk grew more and more. I have lived in this house for decades, never suspecting anything unusual of any kind, yet now I find out some rock (that may be alive) is buried under the cellar. Or rather, our house is built over it to hide it. That revelation wouldn't be so frightening were it not for the vibration it's apparently causing. I didn't really know how to feel -- afraid, lucky, safe, in danger -- maybe it was a good thing, protecting us from some unknown evil. Or maybe it was incubating down there, in the dirt, in the dark, awaiting the day when it would... what? Hatch? Explode? Dig its way out and say "Hello"?

But I had to break away. Hours on the phone had left me with cauliflower ear, and I rubbed it to restore normality. Every half hour or so while I was on the phone, Binky had appeared in front of me holding a sign which said "Let's get flower arch from the high school", and each time I nodded, waving him away as each time his face screwed up in frustration. He wanted me to drop the phone and rush out the door.

After a quick call to the high school administration office, I received permission to get the Arch O' Flowers that was sitting behind the gym, near the dumpsters. I felt silly asking for their trash, but the nice lady seemed to understand and welcomed our offer to take it off their hands. Apparently the sanitation dept. wouldn't.

The high school was only five blocks away, so I gathered the boys and we set out walking to get the thing. It was constructed of PCV pipe and colored tissue paper, peaking at about eight feet high, so we should be able to carry it home. I anticipated minor repair and clean up on it, but it should make a nice photo spot outside our clubhouse. I mentioned as much, and got no argument from the boys. Our plan was to photograph our 100,000th subscriber standing under it, but as yet we hadn't heard back from the winner. A minor detail.

A light rain had splashed our neighborhood a bit earlier, and with the cloud cover keeping us cool, we enjoyed the walk. The houses in our neighborhood were set far back on large lots, mostly fully fronted with trees and bushes, providing lots of privacy for the owners. Walking down our street was nearly like following a paved path in the woods.

It didn't take long for the questions to start:

"Is our house going to vibrate apart?" "Can we put a tuning fork on the humming column and see what frequency it is?" "If we tied a string between the vibrating pole and another pole will the string jiggle real fast?" "How can we attach a motor to it and harness that power for free energy?"

But I took this statement from Linky very seriously: "We should get the ground-penetrating radar from the Geology Dept. at the university and see what's buried there."

As of yet, I hadn't told the boys anything else about what I had learned in my father's journal, beyond that which I had read aloud to them. The didn't know about the rock, or about the cryptic story of its prehistoric activities, nor the bombshell that Aunt Purl laid on me suggesting strongly that the rock is buried under our house. I wasn't ready to tell them, and I didn't. But Linky's comment about the ground-penetrating radar got me to thinking, and I only half heard the rest of the babble as we walked. I knew some of my father's old colleagues at the university. They were all old men now, like me, and had actually been his assistants or students way back then. Unfortunately, all of his contemporaries had passed away. I wondered for a moment if any of them had left behind a hidden journal, too, but dismissed it. I would never know. But if one or two of the scholars who worked with my father who still lived in town could be intrigued enough to quietly use some equipment to get a picture of what lay beneath the cellar, well, it might be worth bringing them in on this mystery.

I was still weighing all that in my mind when we reached the high school. Dinky sprinted ahead as soon as the arch of flowers could be seen leaning against the back brick wall of the gym building, and Linky and Binky immediately took off after him. Long before I reached the group, they had hoisted it on their shoulders and were carrying it toward me, looking like a small army of ants carrying a giant toenail clipping.

"Well, isn't that sweet?" I commented, walking around the arch of flowers. It was still in great condition, and fortunately the light rain we've had recently didn't damage it noticeably.

"It's a beauty, isn't it, Uncle Url!" Binky gushed, obviously quite proud he had found this gem. "It's going to be great-looking outside our clubhouse!"

"Isn't there a brace or feet or something for it?" I asked, looking around the ground in a vast sweep, "there's something over there. Wait." I walked over next to the wall to pick up what was obviously some bracing material for the arch, a back foot and a front foot for both sides, made from the same PVC piping material. All we had to do was screw it on. I bent down to grab them when I noticed a vine had wrapped around it. I pulled hard, anticipating breaking the vine, but no luck. I bent down to look closer -- the vine had grown straight up out of the concrete. Just like that. It had punctured the unbroken concrete and continued it's march upward, finding the pipe and wrapping around it tightly. I stood, retrieved my pocket knife, and bent to cut it. It cut easily and was quite moist inside, but otherwise, it appeared to be a normal vine, but with no leaves of any kind. As I lifted the bracing material, I noticed several other places around the back of the building with vines growing right up through the concrete road.

The walk back carrying the arch of flowers didn't go unnoticed by several drivers and a few pedestrians. Most folks in this area recognized Linky, Dinky and Binky by sight, and although they always give a friendly wave, no one ever engages them in conversation much.

We found a good spot for the Arch, and the boys each took turns posing underneath it, and then ran to the house to make a sign for it (I was sure it would be gaudy).

While they were otherwise entertained, I started for my office to read some more from my father's journal... but in passing through the living room, I felt or heard or was otherwise oddly turned to the door leading to the cellar. I stopped walking, looked at the cellar door for several seconds, remembering the hum, the buried rock, the whole thing... and I knew I had to take another look, maybe to find a bump in the ground or something else that would indicate a secret buried beneath the soil.

Pulling the cellar key from my pocket from where I had put it this morning, I turned the lock, grabbing the flashlight Linky had left on the ledge, and headed down the stairs. The cellar seemed the same as before, and of course I walked over and laid a hand upon the vibrating support pole. Still humming. I decided to carefully examine the edges of the floor at the walls all around the cellar, looking for any secret switch or hidden compartment or anything unusual, and then work my way back to the center of the room.

I stumbled on something. Recovering, I aimed the flashlight toward it, and gasped. A vine. Or maybe a root. Something sticking a few inches right up out of the soil. Remembering what I had found outside the gym, and how it had wrapped around a pipe, after emerging from hard concrete, I panicked. Flaring the flashlight all around the cellar's dirt floor, I saw dozens of them... dark, pointy root-like vine things emerging from the ground. They had not been there this morning. Quickly growing terror leaped into my throat and I knew something awful was happening -- whatever was buried beneath the cellar had been disturbed, it wasn't happy or quiet or asleep anymore, and it was active. I saw a tiny splash of dirt move out of the corner of my, I immediately turned the flashlight to it, and saw another one pluck itself above ground, wiggling slightly.

I ran to the cellar steps and stormed up them quickly, slamming the door behind me. My mind was too excited and frightened to think clearly. This thing was on the move -- into our house -- and if it was the same thing I found at the high school, emitting tentacles from the same body, that would mean it had a reach that extended at least five blocks to the high school, all underground!

My God -- how big is it? And Grampa Url knew about this thing?

CHAPTER SEVEN

I didn't know what to do. Who would? I couldn't call the police just because some roots started coming up in the cellar; what's the threat? "Officer, I believe those roots are actually something else, and they will eventually grow to strangle the house and all within it, and furthermore, you should know they are growing all over town, and will certainly strangle civilization as we know it." It sounded silly, and I shuttered at the thought of the loony bin I'd be placed. They'd Baker Act me, for my own protection. I could leave the boys alone for a few days if I nailed shut every drawer and locked every cabinet, but I couldn't leave them for weeks. Besides, I really only had suspicions, and those had come from an old journal written decades in the past.

Nevertheless, the "roots" or tentacles or whatever were still there, and on the move.

I figured I had a few hours before I needed to take a definite action, either to move out of the house, or call some authorities when the roots reached the stairwell, or seek emergency help from the University's biology or geology departments, or both. Or all three.

Double-checking to make sure the cellar door was locked, I hustled up to my office and bolted myself in. Glancing out the

---

window, I saw the boys busily addressing the matter of decorating the Clubhouse entrance for our 100,000th subscriber party, were it to, in fact, ever take place. Linky was balanced precariously on a step ladder, reaching heroically beyond his center of gravity to hammer home a nail attaching the Flower Arch to the clubhouse's entrance roof. Binky was holding the ladder steady for him, but his attention was obviously on trying to swat away Dinky who was attempting to tape flowers to Binky's head. A pile of colorful Magic Markers and lots of posterboard and cardboard boxes lay scattered around.

They'd be at this project for a while.

So I had time to read more of the journal, perhaps to find instructions or answers or explanations or something which would give me an idea of what to do about the growing thing under the house.

I pulled open the journal at the bookmark where I had finished reading last, and turned the page.

It was blank.

I turned another blank page, then another, counting 5 in all, until I reached another page titled "SCHEMATIC". It was formulas. All weird chemical formulas using words I'd never seen before. Impossible words like annulate lamellae, ribosome, vermicule, middle and posterior lamella, mosaic egg, plastogene, neurofilament, nucleocytoplasmic ratio, hemidesmosome, diastema, diploid... it went on and on. Numbers, fractions, weird symbols. Scientific jargon at it's worst.

I couldn't understand a single word except "DNA" and "RNA" and then lower on the page these two paragraphs:

A nucleic acid that carries the genetic information in the cell and is capable of self-replication and synthesis of RNA. DNA consists of two long chains of nucleotides twisted into a double helix and joined by hydrogen bonds between the complementary bases adenine and thymine or cytosine and guanine. The sequence of nucleotides determines individual hereditary characteristics. A polymeric constituent of all living cells and many viruses, consisting of a long, usually single-stranded chain of alternating phosphate and ribose units with the bases adenine, guanine, cytosine, and uracil bonded to the ribose. The structure and base sequence of RNA are determinants of protein synthesis and the transmission of genetic information. The need to have proteins already present in order to assemble the molecules whose job it is to assemble proteins in the first place has become an intractable "chicken and egg" problem. Neither RNA or DNA can exist without the other, but how did either one evolve without the other already present? I shall attempt to prove that both RNA and DNA were introduced to the earth's biosystem from an external source.

I thought I understood that last part, but I had to read it again very slowly...

Neither RNA or DNA can exist without the other, but how did either one evolve without the other already present? I shall attempt to prove that both RNA and DNA were introduced to the earth's biosystem from an external source.

I had to force myself to believe. The logic was interesting, but never before had anyone proven any such thing. I only knew what everybody knew about DNA; DNA was the intricate coding system that told each life form how to grow, mature, thrive, and I guess, die. Without the DNA blueprint replicated from parent to child, no species would reproduce. Or exist, either, I guessed. But I remembered, of course, that Grampa Url had written this journal in the years immediately following the turn of the century in 1900, yet, the discovery of RNA and DNA wasn't until the 1950's.

Impossible to fathom, no matter how long I tried to let it sink in.

I kept turning pages, searching each jumble of writing for something intelligible. Scientists would probably find this data intriguing, if not earth-shattering, but to me, it was mostly gobbledygook.

And then I found something -- a hand-drawn diagram, penned on heavier paper, almost like canvas, and stitched into one of the journal pages with needle and thread. An antique typewriter had been used, clumsily, to add a description to the diagram of the earth:

```
The earth's mantle extends like a shell
thousands of miles deep. The lair of the Beast
is in it. Each Rock-Beast lies hundreds of miles
below the surface. All communication is effected
through sinewy tenticles too numerous to count.
```

Well that cleared up the Rock/Beast issue. They were real, and one of them was underneath our ever-loving house.

"Golly!" I chuckled aloud to myself, "That's a fine how-do-you-do!" The shock of all this finally jelled into a real understanding in my mind and it had made me silly. Surely a mental breakdown was near. "Heck," I said again to myself, "death is close at hand. That's different!" I was grinning madly without knowing it. "What's for dinner?" I cackled insanely, raising my face to the ceiling, just laughing for lack of anything else to do. "Here a rock, there a rock, everywhere a rock rock. Rocks that live, rocks that thrive, rocks right on our block!" I was definitely losing it.

But fear quickly regained the upper hand: "SO THEN WHY DID YOU BUILD THE HOUSE RIGHT ON TOP OF ONE!" I screamed at the Journal, trying to rebuke my father for bringing all this upon us. I slammed the book shut and threw it across to the couch. Numb, enraged, afraid and sad all at the same time, I sat with head in hands, eyes closed, not awake, not asleep, just conscious. That was all.

I heard my name and realized I had forgotten about the boys outside. I turned to look out the window as more shouts and unintelligible yelling poured in, muted by the shut window.

My eyes zoomed in on Dinky, his arms flailing, with Linky and Binky dancing around him, swatting sticks or something at his feet. Dinky was pulling and shaking and trying to jump all at once, yet his feet never left the ground.

A root was wrapped around his ankles, and it wasn't letting go.

Time was up.

CHAPTER EIGHT

At some point, during my rush out of the office, before I fumbled with the lock on my office door, I had grabbed the letter opener from my desk. As a weapon? As a cutting device? I didn't know, but since the letter opener was in my hand as I flew down two flights of stairs on my way to save Dinky, I would use it as best I could, inadequate as it might be.

At the bottom of the last stair, I grabbed the banister with my right hand and did the same sling-shot move I've yelled at the boys for doing. The old banister creaked and swayed, but held firm as my forward momentum was whipped 180 degrees, swinging me toward the back door of the house.

Trying not to slide into the walls while quick-stepping over the scattered throw rugs peppering our hardwood flooring, I reached the back door and flung it open... and crashed right into Linky and Dinky and Binky like a bowling ball against a tight 3-pin spare, who simultaneously were trying to get into the house.

"What the..." I cursed as the bodies tumbled to the ground. I landed directly on Binky, and his "oomph!" was the loudest noise I heard, since my ear was directly over his mouth on the way down. Of course, I had expected to be darting across the lawn to rescue Dinky from the roots gripping him to the ground... and I was carrying a sharp implement. I focused on my left hand, and there it was, lying harmlessly on the ground.

"A giant worm attacked me and almost killed me!" Dinky started shouting, "I fought it off and Linky didn't even help me!" "You're only alive now because of me, dork!" Linky countered, "I'm the one who scared it back into the ground!"

Their hysterical voices pounded my eardrums for a minute or two, and I won't trouble you with the various points, counterpoints, accusations and retorts, but the short story is that "something" appearing to be a root or a worm had launched up from the sod, entwined Dinky's feet and ankles in a tight grip, and then suddenly relaxed and retreated back into the ground. They wanted me to go over and look at the scene of the emergency, and I considered it, but then thought better of it: "Let's get off this grass right now." and I shooed the boys into the house.

Suddenly quieted by the realization that merely standing on our own lawn wasn't safe, the boys just stood in the living room, fearful expressions on their faces, starting at me for an answer, or some guidance. Circumstances were changing so fast I didn't have time to grow accustomed to any of these turn of events, and my stomach was becoming queasy.

"Alright boys, listen up." I started, breathing hard, but mustering a tone of confidence which I didn't really feel. "We've got a situation here, and it's time I explained it to you. At least, as much as I know." I sat down on the couch, expecting them to also sit. They didn't.
"We're all gonna die!" Dinky screamed at the top of his lungs,

diving behind the high-backed stuffed chair near the corner of the room (that had been one of his favorite hiding places for years). Binky slowly sat on the floor, trying to use his arms to support him, but then just gently laid prone on the floor and closed his eyes. He was out cold.

Only Linky sat down normally, ignoring the histrionics of his siblings, and looked at me solemnly. "We have to dig up the cellar." he finally stated.

"Or move," I added quickly, half chuckling. Sitting back in the sofa, I rubbed my face and eyes with my hands. I had already decided to spill the beans to Linky, but I was sluggish in starting the process.

But I did. I brought him up to date on the Journal, about the DNA/RNA chicken-and-egg story, the diagram of all the rocks buried deep around the planet, the communication between the rocks and the roots and the primitives (and theoretically every life-form living today). I told him about Aunt Purl's memory of Grampa Url saying something was hidden under the house, the roots that started to grow through the dirt in the cellar, and how some how, in some way, Grampa Url knew all about it, and for some reason relished it. Reveled in it. It was his secret life's work, like he had discovered electricity or something.

But why, we did not know. No happy ending occurred to me, or to Linky, and we discussed the details as we knew them for a several minutes, until Linky asked "I wonder how much they've grown in the cellar?"

I thought about that. About half an hour had passed since I ran like a banshee from the cellar. There's no telling what was happening now... however, since the roots had retreated in the back yard, maybe they had retreated from the cellar as well.

"We have to know," Linky continued. "If the rock-with-roots thing is about to hatch and start covering the world, we know it's starting from our cellar, and since Grampa Url knew it was there, isn't it our responsibility to understand it? The answers may still be revealed in the rest of the Journal you haven't read yet. This root-sprouting might be going on all over the world right now, not just here."

I just stared at Linky, wondering how he suddenly got so smart. I listened to his logic, and though I agreed, I said nothing. Perhaps it was much easier for him, being so much younger, to digest and be comfortable with the idea of an unknown entity buried under the house. The MTV generation. They expect things like this to happen, and are probably disappointed when it doesn't.

"Alright," I said, standing slowly, "let's go take a look." Linky stood with me, and I carefully stepped over Binky, noting his chest still moved with every breath. He was OK. We both could hear Dinky whimpering the entire time, and I was content to let hiding Dinkys hide.

Again armed with a flashlight, I led the way slowly down the steps to the cellar, my eyes adjusting quickly. I stopped on the bottom step, wary of committing to the dirt floor to provide safe footing. Sweeping the flashlight around the dungeon-like room, I quickly saw the hole. In the center of the room, the sides sloping into a pit of darkness like a gigantic throat, roots had apparently weaved a flattened pattern around the hole to form its frightening shape, which measured at least five feet in diameter and obviously led deep into the ground. The roots looked knitted, and the fear I had felt earlier overcame me, and I didn't notice as my legs crumpled underneath me and I flopped down into a sitting position. I had often read the description "waves of nausea" in novels, but now I was feeling it rip apart my stomach.

And I vomited.

A shadowy mass moved quickly past my right side, and with uncaring eyes I watched Linky tiptoe closer and closer to the hole. He was now carrying the flashlight, shining it all round the grotesque orifice, but I had no idea when or how he had taken it out of my grip. He knelt to study something in the dirt near his feet, holding the flashlight close to brightly light something. He moved the beam toward the hole, then back to his feet, and then back to the hole, and then he stood.

And he laughed!

"Uncle Url!" Linky called, the humor ringing through his voice quite clearly. "You're not going to believe it! Come look at this!" I looked up into Linky 's face, incredulous at how calm -- in fact how happy -- he was. His face beamed, obviously having learned something that counterbalanced the fact that a GAPING HOLE OF DEATH had opened up in our cellar. I didn't move, and with my eyes drooping, the strength long since sapped from my body, I shook my head No.

Linky nonchalantly walked over to where I sat on the stairs and held out a hand. "Come on, Uncle," he said gently, even kindly, "let me help you up." We struggled with that for a minute, and with much ado I finally came to my feet, grasping the handrail as tight as I could, which wasn't very.

"Come look at what I found. It's a message from Grampa Url," he said, continuing a smile that I must admit, strengthened me quite a bit.

"What? A message from..." and the rest garbled off as I finished the sentence in my head, its meaning simply impossible. But Linky understood me, and kept tugging me toward the spot in the dirt, near the edge of the throat in the ground. We finally hobbled to the correct spot, my resistance growing as we drew closer to the hole, and he shined the flashlight directly onto a patch in the dirt.

And indeed, I was looking at words. Words formed from tiny tentacles, slender roots approximately the width of yarn, and they twisted and turned and looped around in very distinct shapes. Letters, in English. It was a message!

I stooped closer, squinting to read the words through the uneven light, the harsh shadows made it difficult, but I could still make it out:

DEAR LINKY DINKY BINKY AND URL
WELCOME TO MY LABORATORY
GRAMPA

And there lay the letter opener I had left outside, now pointing directly toward the hole.

CHAPTER NINE

Ramford Url stood far forward on deck, as close as he could to the bow of the giant wooden ship and still maintain solid footing, as the vessel plowed through the viciously black and angry waters of the North Atlantic. Huge coils of thick rope occupied the v-shaped area of the deck near the proud bowsprit, which in turn held firm the stays for the fore-topmast sails and jibs. Short lengths of wood and iron and brass were placed in uniformed positions on the deck, keeping the running rigging secured, but became a treacherous field for anyone wishing to not trip and fall across the violently swaying deck. Ramford kept a wary eye on the heavy piece of curved timber projecting from his starboard position as it valiantly held the anchor in place. For it to break loose, the anchor would pound a deadly hole into side of the ship, and since the HMS Kalhoon was now 15 days away from port, aid would not be forthcoming.

Freezing salt water sprayed the decks and all souls upon it at every downward thrust of the hull as the seas continued in relentless turmoil. Ramford closed his eyes and turned his head in anticipation of every splash of frigid water, and wished mightily for a higher perch, but knew none were to be had. With one eye on the roiling seas, and another on the seemingly fragile ship's rigging, he peered through squinted eyes for land (or icebergs or other ships or floating debris) or anything that might be of dire interest to a ship's captain in a storm. Only 22 crew manned this aging 90-foot vessel, and if loyalty could be the only factor leading to success, this secret voyage would be a smashing victory. But all hands knew a vessel this size required at least 50 skilled sailors to manage God's oceans with confidence, and the brave 22 counted on Luck as being the extra hands.

As an especially large wave crested the bulwark and hit Ramford with a veracity that nearly washed him across the deck, he again mentally cursed this expedition, it's incomplete preparation and even the foolhardy nature of the mission. Surely a better way could be found to travel the seas, and he had often wished someone would continue the work of DaVinci by developing a mechanical contrivance that could master the skies as birds do so effortlessly. Peace and tranquility lived in harmony only a few feet above these violent black seas, so why couldn't Man float on columns of air like gulls and avoid this wet hell?

But he held on, both physically and emotionally, and did his best to finish his watch without being swept into the maelstrom, one of several which would whip the North Atlantic this year of our Lord, 1888.

The storm dissipated a few hours later, conveniently in time for the part-time ship's cook to serve a fine spread for a ravished crew. The crew's bawdy conversations during the meal always centered around speculation as to the true mission of this vessel, and why it must be undermanned, and why such an old ship was outfitted on a shoestring budget for this mysterious venture. Ramford knew they wondered about his presence, too, but dared not speak of it in his company, since he kept close counsel with the captain. They would never know (he hoped) the true reason he was on board, and even if they did, they would certainly not understand it. So far on this ocean journey the crew had eyed him with speculation, but couldn't fault him on performance of duties. Ramford's days were either spent on deck spying distant horizons, or huddled with the captain on the quarterdeck laboriously studying maps and consulting thick bound journals. The crew knew this area of the North Atlantic had been charted by the Norwegians centuries ago, and in more modern times by the HMS Beagle, Darwin's naturalist voyage, in the 1830's. They knew there was little here to find.

The HMS Kalhoon, recently purchased and overhauled in the expansive dry docks of the Port of London by an American publishing company (Colonial Pen & Press) had raised quite a few eyebrows among the traders and shipping magnates of England of the 1880s. Not understanding why an American firm would bear the additional costs of maintaining a ship across the Atlantic, when the shipyards of Boston served oceangoing vessels quite well for the "colonies", suspicion met every stage of the refit. And Ramford didn't help manners as he tasked throughout the merchants and shopkeeps, ordering supplies and foodstuffs without enlightening those who asked about his purpose or the Kalhoon's charter. But he did pay cash.

The crew had been carefully selected, not only for their individual sailing experience, but also their lack of association with London's maritime community, the logic being if the crew didn't know anybody, they'd be less tempted to talk. Several members were brought over from Boston, others from Italy. The ship's Master had been recently retired, enjoying the fruits of years of loyalty by purchasing a magnificent estate high atop the rocky slopes of Mount Arpeaud on an island in the Bay of Fundy, preferring the cold winters of seclusion to the noisy bother of any city in his beloved Nova Scotia. Once entrusted with the grand purpose of the mission, however, he agreed to head it, although he still demanded double wages. But his lips, too, would be sealed.

And now the Kalhoon plowed through relentless seas, seeking to reach a position 1000 nautical miles east of Greenland's southern tip, her crew doubting the value of the cruise as the stormy weather dropped in temperature faster than a degree per hour. Soon, the scattered small icebergs would give way to giant floating mountains of ice, as deadly as they were glorious.

Once the Kalhoon slipped into the Rockall Rise, three weeks northwest of Ire land's Mizen Head, she turned due West, making a bead on the Iceland Basin. This empty patch of the North Atlantic Ocean, 800 or so miles south of Iceland proper, was known for its mathematical perfection on the map of the planet, rather than it's open water. Residing on the 60 degree parallel it stood out only as a landmark on the compass. At certain times of the year, swordfishermen would venture out this far if the waters were lean closer to home, but other than transatlantic cargo ships, these waters were unremarkable.

In the relative calm, cold as it was, a few of the crew stood around the deck, wondering what would happen now that they'd arrived. The horizon was clearly visible without a spyglass, the gentle curve of the edge of the earth making all who saw it wonder why people hadn't deduced the world was round eons before they did. The

Kalhoon was at full stop, bobbing in wait at the invisible coordinates.

"So this is what we're paid not to talk about, eh?" one of the hands commented to another as they stood against the bulwark, mindlessly gnawing on a grift of jerky. "A fool's errand, I'd say," his companion commented in return. "Are we looking for a sea monster? Keep an eye out -- maybe ole 'Nessy will show herself!" and they laughed at the prospect. With no wind and with orders from the captain to remain at stationkeeping, the crew had little to do but gossip, chew and cuss.

Ramford Url was pacing the tiny deck of the quartermaster's post, arguing fiercely with the captain, and it was the captain's turn to argue back: "I can't say how long they'll wait," he tried to explain impatiently. "The men are sailors, they need to sail. Floating around an empty sea for no apparent reason will drive them to fight, or worse."

"We stay," Ramford ordered. "I've paid for passage to this location, and we've rations and good health to stay for five weeks. The crew is your responsibility, you handle them!"

The captain was not accustomed to accepting orders from a civilian, and wasn't going to start now. "You've paid a mighty fine fee, Mr. Url, there's no debating that point. But you've paid for passage to this spot in the sea, and it's a wild goose chase after a mysterious island I don't believe exists, and you've paid for passage back to the States." He quieted, leaned forward and stared directly into Ramford's eyes, "You did not pay for a mutiny, and that's what you'll get if we sit here for no reason for five weeks!"

"There is reason," Ramford replied steadily, "a very good reason, and it shouldn't take five weeks. But if it does, then keep yourself armed and ready to shoot. I will be!" Ramford slid back the gate of his heavy coat to reveal a pearl-handled six-shot, waited for the captain's eyes to drop to his waist to see it, then turned on his heel and left the room.

Ramford made his way down a few steps, bobbing and weaving as the deck slanted and tilted beneath him but his finely tuned sense of balance served him well; he had earned at least that over the last two weeks on seas more wicked than these. Making his way to the bow, Ramford passed several crewman, nodding and grunting recognition as is the way of men.

The wind had picked up, and its cold bite rattled Ramford and he wrapped his coat tighter and re-buttoned it as he trampled up the steep deck forward. Near the bow, he was surprised to see the old man standing there, looking outward at the horizon.
"Charles!" Ramford called, quickening his pace to meet up with his friend. "You'll catch your death! I shan't be nursing you!"

The old man turned to recognize Ramford approaching, lifted up his head to laugh at the remark, began to cough, collected himself for a moment, then stuffed his long beard back into his coat to keep the salt spray from mangling it with moisture.

"This is the place, you needn't worry," Charles Darwin replied to his friend, "I am beginning to smell it's scent."

CHAPTER TEN

For eleven days the HMS Kalhoon bobbed on the icy waters, drifting and rotating slowing in the changing winds, the crew counting the sun's passage across the blue sky and marking time each night with the effusive spread of starlight across the night's dark ceiling. The Captain checked his ship's position studiously each pre-dawn morning with the sextant and plotted a correcting course for the day's brief sail back to the proper coordinates, a routine which continued each and every day of the wait.

The Captain kept the men busy in ship-bound toil at every first light, as if the ship were being prepared for a voyage, rather than already underway. His daily inspections found every torn sail, splintered deckwood, broken hinge, frayed rope and unclean surface wherever it was on the ship, and ordered it repaired. Every rusty spot was sanded clean, each slithering crack to be resealed and waterproofed, every square yard of open deck to be oiled, and when the seas calmed the most, a makeshift lift was fashioned to hoist men down the sides of the hull to inspect for cleavage along the rigid sides of the ship and effect repair. After a few days, the rigging had never been tighter on this old craft, and the sails never more crisply maintained. It was a stellar example of a "tight ship."

But each afternoon the grueling upkeep of the ship was called off, affording the men several remaining hours of daylight for sport.

Some boxed bare knuckled, the sailors wagering on the outcome; others fished, fashioning hooks and using a lightweight rope as fishing line, experimenting with various cured meats from the galley as bait until the first giant Cod was snared, then using its liver and other colorful internal organs as bait, landing even more oversized deep sea finned beasts. After one particularly successful day of fishing, the Captain cautiously granted permission for a wooden spit to be built on the afterdeck. The Cook rubbed the white flanks of meat with salt and seared enormous slabs of what the men called Sea Bass, but whether it was or not would never be known. It was a feast for all but two of the men, who stood by with pails of water to prevent a shipboard fire.

With no purpose to fill the nights, the crew frequently wished upon the stars. It wasn't known to the sailors or anyone else on board the Kalhoon that very few of the bright points in the sky were stars; most of the lights in the sky were actually galaxies, each a spinning circle of billions of individual suns. Only in the tightly knit band of light that belted the southern sky could individual stars to be seen, as they comprised the Milky Way galaxy. Galaxies, stars, planets, it didn't matter, the sailors wished upon them anyway.

The night held a fascination for sailors, who read into each funny appearance of light in the sky as a remarkable sign from God, or some Goddess, or any other heavenly power. They figured lights in the sky as a good omen, or a bad omen, or some other message portending the future, its meaning usually always open for inter-pretation. Shooting stars, particularly, were carefully watched for, as they were unanimously understood to be a sign of good luck for sailors, and since the nightly average was two or three (as long as the skies were clear) it helped keep up moral. Perhaps a wise old Captain started the ancient fable that shooting stars were a messenger of good luck, and by calling it so, it became so.

In the not so distant future, perhaps 80 years or so, the skies would begin filling with manmade satellites until tens of thousands of objects were circling the earth, easily visible as straight-moving bright spots to sailors of the future who peered from the ocean's black surface. Invisible beams of radiation, harmless of course, in the form of radio transmissions and microwaves and Very Low Frequency underwater beacons, and television signals and a dozen other types of radiating waves all crisscrossing past each other directly through every cubic yard of earth's atmosphere. Even a long wire would be laid, unbroken, across the floor of the Atlantic, and telephone service would begin between the two continents. But in 1888 there was none of that. The ether was empty.

Ramford Url kept a tight watch on the aging Charles Darwin during these days of stationkeeping, and they stayed below decks as much as possible. The man was a legend in the making, but word of his travels and discoveries were not yet world renown. His five year Voyage of the Beagle had taken place over 50 years prior to this journey, and still only the academics were privy to his astonishing and revolutionary discoveries. But it was for exactly that reason this trip was possible, and necessary -- Darwin hadn't revealed everything he discovered, because it wasn't yet fully explored. Now, with his friend Ramford Url's help (and money from another publishing friend at Colonial Pen & Press) this second, secret voyage was underway, albeit 50 years late.

The HMS Kalhoon was a large ship, but not large enough to halt gossip about the elderly gentlemen with the long beard. Fortune kept the secret of Darwin's fame, because the sailors, including the Captain, were not educated enough or attentive to current science news enough to know who the man was, and if they did, he would probably be keel-hauled for his obscene suggestions that God had not created anything, but rather Nature had cleverly evolved itself into higher life forms. The sailors would have no take with that! A man who profaned God's creation would make them a target for disaster, jinxing the ship, and the resulting riot would have Darwin gurgling in the cold waters as shark food within minutes, probably with the Captain providing the decisive push.

But neither the sailors nor the Captain knew anything of the old man's ideas, and as such were content to ignore him, satisfied that he was Ramford's advisor on this journey, and since it was Ramford who footed the expense for this voyage, he was treated as some-thing of a Ship's Master too.

Floating around a desolate patch of the North Atlantic for nearly half a month had started a growing tension among the crew, so much so that Ramford and Darwin took to the decks for fresh air only during chow, to avoid confrontation, when the men were below for the evening meal. Their sunset strolls around the deck, peering off toward the horizon, searching for an object no other soul on board believed to exist became increasingly tense for the two scientists as well. Ramford fought back his own doubts as he queried the elder genius over and over again about their mission. Darwin never faltered in his confidence, at least openly, and this evening was no different. They finished their circumnavigation of the deck for a fifth time when they heard the approaching raucous voices of the crew climbing topside after their meal.

"...aye, lads, but the mermaids will swoon after one gaze upon me mighty arms!" a sailor was saying with all the braggadocio he could muster, flexing his right arm in demonstration. The continual babble of the sailors continued, until one saw the two scientists standing against the rail eyeing them warily. "Have ye found our mermaids yet?" he called over, laughing, "I need some extry warmth in me bunk tonight!" The laughter continued, but something about the expression of disgust on Ramford's face at the ignorant jokes of the sailors didn't sit well with one of the crustier men, and he sauntered over to where they stood.

"How long will you be keeping us here, with nothing to do but wait for your fancy to show up?" He stood solid, glaring at Ramford, demanding an answer. Darwin was visibly intimidated, frightfully watching the angry demeanor and the dirty, rough appearance of this seasoned sailor. This man was the ship's victor in the boxing matches and the purple cuts in the flesh around his deeply tanned and stubbled face were his badges of honor to prove it. "We want to know how long," the sailor added as more of a growl than a statement.

But when the sailor took a small step forward, Ramford moved in front of Darwin to shield him and stared down at the sailor, thankful the salty boxer was shorter than he. "When we find what we're looking for," Ramford fired back forcefully, "you and the rest of the crew will be getting your bonus. Until then, consider yourself on holiday!" The two locked eyes for several long moments, but when Ramford let a small smile form on his face, it broke the tension, and the sailor turned to his shipmates with a flare of his arm and a wide grin, announcing "That's it, men! We're all on Holiday! Break out the Rum!" The group exploded in laughter again, and en masse turned toward the bow and moved off, some to check their fishing lines, others to start their watch.

Darwin watched the group leave and waited until they were well out of earshot. "You handled him well," Darwin complimented Ramford Url, who didn't answer, but continued to study the distant horizon.

After a relatively relaxing period, watching the sun set in a silent orange explosion in one direction and the sky gently darken in the other, the two walked along the ship toward their cabin for a bit of reading by lamplight before retiring. Ramford would dutifully write in his journal again, trying to find another way of stating: "Nothing is happening."

Dusk was nearly at hand.

"We don't have a lot of time, Charles" Ramford said as they walked along the deck. "Another week, maybe, but that's all. These men will surely stop caring about a bonus when winter starts to set in, and the Captain said a cold snap will soon be upon us."

The two continued to watch the seas as they neared the doorway. Froth bounced and banged against the hull of the ship as the seas of the North Atlantic grew more boisterous.

Suddenly Darwin shouted above the rising noise of the wind, "It won't be long, LOOK..." he was pointing off to starboard to an object floating in the water. It was tubular in shape, appearing to be made of wood, very slender, like a snake, at least the length of two men. It wiggled briefly against the constant wake of the seas, then darted below the surface. Ramford saw it. "A sea snake of some kind" he said.

"No," Darwin replied. "that's no snake. That's a scout. A fragment of the real thing. You'll see. I reckon we'll get a personal introduction in a short while." He nodded to Ramford, clenched his coat tighter around him, and turned to go below deck.

Ramford called after Darwin, stepping to catch up with the older scientist. "Is that what you saw last time? Before the first contact?"

"Not exactly." Darwin shouted back. "Last time I caught it in a net and it explained things to me!" Darwin turned to flash a mischievous smile then disappeared below deck.

CHAPTER ELEVEN

Ramford blinked rapidly to regain the moisture in his eyes, and deliberately yawned to gather tears to sharpen his vision. He felt the subtle but soothing flow from his tear ducts as it wet his puffy and dry eyeballs, and the blur began to clear. He seriously examined the darkened cabin, attempting to identify his surroundings. He reckoned it must be between two and five a.m., and he wasn't at all sure why he had just awakened.

Peering through the murky darkness at Darwin's bunk, he tried without success to discern the shape of the scientist beneath the wool blanket, but in the nearly absolute blackness he just couldn't decide one way or the other if a body lay on that bed. He felt around for the matchsticks he was sure he left on the side table, but he couldn't find them, so he pushed aside his own blanket and crept toward the porthole, stopping to lay a gentle hand on Darwin's bunk. Feeling nothing except soft fabric, he reached for the porthole and flicked aside the lash and pushed out the covering. A modest amount of moonlight immediately brightened the sleeping quarters, and he turned his head to see for sure: Darwin's bunk was definitely empty.

Dressing quickly (and warmly, since the open porthole had almost instantly made the cabin like an icebox), Ramford went in search of the aging scientist. Where would a 77 year-old misunderstood genius go in the middle of a frigid night on a ship with nothing to see or do? With the open porthole now enabling him to see around his cramped quarters, Ramford found the matchsticks, lit the lantern and left the room. Winding his way through the narrow hallways and awkward staircases, he finally escaped the bowels of the ship and reached the forecastle exit.

Peering around the bow he saw only the bright moon and a sky radiant with stars. Hunching a bit in the cold, he started a tour of the ship, hoping to either find the crewman on watch (to ask about which way Darwin went) or to find Darwin himself, and summarily drag him back to bed. So Ramford began his march along the decks.

Up only a few hours before, Darwin had refused to enlighten Ramford on any more of the details of what, exactly, lay ahead, and they had snuffed the lantern and turned in for the night with nothing more being said. The "sea snake" they both saw in the waves off the ship last evening had signalled to Darwin that the encounter with what he had called "the beast" was about to begin, but what that meant, or how dangerous that was to be, remained unspoken.

Ramford was a relative newcomer to this search for the mysterious beast, and didn't have the benefit of Darwin's decades of biological research. When Darwin had contacted Ramford two years ago, it had been to elicit his aid in locating an "anomalistic life form", and to help fund and launch an expedition into the North Atlantic to locate it. As head of the Natural Sciences division at his University, Ramford had no small amount of notoriety himself within scientific circles, and was enthralled to meet with the famed

Evolutionist and to lock resources with him in a joint venture.

Throughout the two years of raising capital and assembling the expedition, Ramford was left with little to go on except his faith in Darwin's reputation and the mysterious exuberance he demonstrated to seek out this new life form. And now, on the eve of their long-awaited discovery, wasn't it time to fully inform his partner about all he knew?

Ramford trudged along the slippery deck. He hadn't noticed it while below, but now with only the sky above his head, it struck him: the ship wasn't moving. Not one whit. It was rock solid and unswaying, which was extremely odd since he could feel the cold winds of the North Atlantic blowing steadily, and often gusting enough to fluff his overcoat despite how tightly he held it closed. Ramford grabbed the rail and looked straight down, attempting to check the condition of the seas below, but could see only blackness. The moon illuminated the other side of the Kalhoon, leaving the starboard in dark shadows.

"Raaamforrrrd!" came a call from a great distance, the sound buffeted about by the unseen forces of nature. Jumping at hearing his name, Ramford whipped his head to and fro, attempting to decipher the direction from whence it originated. "Raaamforrrrd!" the call came again, and he turned his head astonished to find the source coming from the water. Another vessel? Who on board could possibly know him by name (or by sight, for that matter, wrapped up against the cold on this gloomy night?)

Ramford aimed his shout at the sea, "Helllllooo!" studying the distance where the horizon should be, but it was like staring into a black wall.

"Hold a bit, I'll come closer!" the voice returned, and with that Ramford grew truly confused, and a bit frightened. Another ship large enough to be sailing this part of the Atlantic should not be brazenly approaching the Kalhoon at night without several crew members attending to the approach with ropes and prods and bumpers. He quickly looked around the deck for the nightwatch, but still no one else stirred on board. Ramford wasn't exactly sure what to do, so he called back as clearly and as loudly as he could into the darkness."Wait! I'm the only one on deck. I can't help you approach by myself. Let me fetch the Captain!"

"Don't get the Captain, are you mad?" the voice answered, now closer and much lower. Ramford focused down into the water, about ten yards off the side of the ship, and gradually saw a bewildering sight: Charles Darwin, his long beard tucked into the front of his overcoat as usual, walking on the still black waters directly toward him.

"And stop shouting, we don't want to wake the crew, you know," Darwin said, having reached the sides of the Kalhoon, now looking straight up at Ramford, who was still staring down at him with mouth open.

"Darwin!" Ramford finally spoke, exasperated, "by all that's holy, what are you doing... down there?"

"It's time, Ramford. It's all ready for us." Darwin gestured out to sea. "Climb down the nets and be quick about it. We'll be burned like witches if the crew rises and sees all this." Darwin moved a few feet to grab the boarding net that stretched alongside the hull of the proud wooden ship, and stuffed a foot in the bottom rung to steady it for Ramford's descent. "Hurry along now!"

"What are you standing on? The water?" Ramford asked, leaning as far over the side as he could to get a better view. "I'm certainly hallucinating!"

"It's the roots, man. There's a nice flooring here just beneath the surface. It runs for hundreds of yards. It's firm and flat. We'll not drown, it's made a way for us." Darwin explained. "But I'm telling you to hurry!"

Only partly believing, but understanding the urgency of this moment of discovery, Ramford hurled a leg over the bulwark and gained purchase on the net. Positioning himself with some confidence, he climbed down the 12 or so feet to the water's surface. At the bottom, he tested the solidity of the flooring with a toe, and after it held his full weight, he released the net and stood next to Darwin.

"How do you know where the roots end and the sea begins? I don't want to fall off an edge into these waters!"

"It's bigger than we'll ever see." Darwin replied, walking off into the darkness. Ramford followed. "It's holding the ship, too, just as if the whole vessel were sitting on a table like a toy."

The two continued their walk further and further away from the

Kalhoon, Ramford falling a bit behind as he tested each footing before taking it. The root-flooring was uneven, and made with many slender wood-like tentacles clenched together like the logs of a raft. It dipped in places, and fear rose in Ramford's throat at times when the water lapped over his ankles, but neither man tripped or faltered.

CHAPTER TWELVE

I struggled with the handheld remote, trying feverishly to plug the vicious funnels as they swarmed all around me. Black and nasty and spinning at a million miles an hour, the lethal funnels swooped around my head, forcing me to constantly duck and twist out of the way. If I were hit by one of these deadly rotating tops they would slice into my skin like a frisbee'd saw blade. With great difficulty and a lot of luck, I managed a few times to use the remote to slap a plug into a one of them, but the damn thing would cough it out and regroup with the others and commence to dive bomb me again. I kept creeping backwards in constant retreat as the situation became hopelessly grim, when suddenly the entire battle scene dissolved and a new reality gripped my attention: I was face down in the dirt.

"Are you all right?" a voice kept asking. Confused by the still strong memory of the dream but unable to deny the sight of dirt mere inches from my eyes, I gradually came to recognize Linky's voice.

As I stirred and lifted my head, I saw Linky hunched over me. "I think you fainted or something, Uncle Url." he said. "Do you feel okay?"

Coming out of the mental fog, I hoisted myself up on one elbow and surveyed the scene. It was coming back to me (the yawning

©Linky & Dinky Enterprises   www.linkydinky.com   Uncle-Url@linkydinky.com

83

hole in our cellar floor being the first, obvious reminder). "How long was I out?" I mumbled.

"Just a couple of minutes," Linky answered, "but don't worry about that. I think this is perfectly safe. The message from Grampa Url proves it! And I touched it, and..."

"We're not going in there," I interrupted. "We don't know what is in there, and I'm not about to risk anybody's life to find out. There is no sane reason on earth to venture into that hole... you'd have to be nuts to go down a strange pit like that! It will close up behind us and we'll be swallowed alive." I cried.

"But I went in already!" Linky countered, "I went down to the curve and looked around the corner while you were passed out. There's a room or something down there with lots of light and I heard voices. I touched the walls and I saw everything. Grampa is in the tunnel! We have to go see him!"

"Oh goodness," I said, barely audible and exasperated. Not only did I have a hole leading straight to hell in my cellar, it had taken over Linky's brain and washed it clean of common sense. The roots attacking people in the yard were enough to make me fear this thing, now my dead and buried father was in Hell, awaiting a friendly visit.

"Feel that?" Linky had his arm out with his hand flat over the entrance of the tunnel. "A breeze. Coming from inside."

I paused a moment, and finding no harm in it, I lifted my hand

and felt the breeze too. It gusted up a bit, and I smelled the sea. A distinct saltwater smell. "The ocean?" I asked, looking at Linky.

"Just touch right here," Linky stretched himself over the lip of the hole, and flat-handed the side of the tunnel. "It's like a psychic thing. I just know we're supposed to go into the hole and Grampa is in there. Feel it, you'll see!"

Shaking my head "No", I fought my way to my feet, brushing the dirt from my pants. I was about to say (with authority) "We're getting out of here" when Linky started sliding into the hole. I saw his face clearly, looking back at me, not afraid at all, but looking a bit startled. I dove to grab at him but he was gone too quick. In a shot, Linky was down the tunnel around the corner and out of sight.

Every muscle of my body clenched like a tight fist and horrible panic flooded over me. I was frozen in fear, my mind blanked by terror. But ,without spending a nanosecond to reason, I plunged into the hole to rescue Linky.

Faster and faster I ran into the hole, throwing up my hands to brace myself so I wouldn't crash into the approaching tight curve. But upon impact, immediately, I calmed. A sense of euphoria pushed out my fear as I realized, somehow, that this hole was a wonderful thing and very safe and my father was waiting for me. I basked in these happy feelings while I caught my breath, and then realized I was touching the sides of the tunnel and experiencing the psychic communique Linky had told me about. Curious, but not afraid, I lifted my hands off the wall and the images and sensations quickly faded. Intrigued, I reached out with one finger to touch the wall again, and marveled at how the feelings and knowledge re-formed in my mind all over again.

Motion out of the corner of my eye turned my attention to the distant light far off at the end of the tunnel, and I saw a dark form moving within it. I knew it must be Linky. I started off at a jog, careful (for now) not to touch the sides of the wall lest my senses be forever hijacked by artificial feelings and thoughts. I called out for Linky several times, the final time being as loud as I could, but I never got an answer.

After what must have been a hundred yards, I stopped, out of breath. I hadn't run like that in years, and if it hadn't been on a modest downhill grade, I wouldn't have made it as far as I did. Heaving for breath, I looked back toward the entrance to find only blackness. The only direction to go was toward the light, so I started walking for a bit, still catching my breath but making forward progress. Where was the room Linky saw? Did it vanish? Where were the voices? The hole was being tricky, moving rooms around and pulling people into it. Whatever was going on, I didn't trust it - - and I didn't touch the walls. I wanted this thing to stay out of my head as long as possible.

After a while I realized, too late, that I was very deep under-ground, and not seeming to get any closer to my goal. The phrase "buried alive" crossed my mind. Linky was nowhere to be found. My thighs ached from the constant jogging, and I plopped myself down to rest a moment.

Suddenly, I started sliding forward! Gaining speed! I felt no friction or rubbing on the floor at all, just acceleration as my butt slid steady and true toward the light. I remembered that Linky was laying down when he was pulled into the tunnel, so that must be it. A prone position gets you a ghostly trolley ride in the tunnel of doom.

Whizzing ever faster, the walls now a rushing blur on the side, the lighted spot down the tunnel started to grow larger as I approached. It would have taken hours to run this far, I thought, ironically thankful for the free ride I was getting.

Abruptly, the ride halted, and I found myself sitting on the floor, cross-legged, staring into the tunnel ahead, still a million miles of tube with no end in sight. It was a bit comforting to be stationary once again, so I continued to sit, wondering what kind of destination this was supposed to be. Did something run out of gas?

Behind me a deep voice said "Son..."

I turned my head and saw him. It was him! My Father! Dead for over 50 years, smiling, breathing, alive, his eyes flaring with amusement. It couldn't be him -- it was him! Impossible, no way. Oh goodness, he was younger than me! He appeared every bit as he did in many of the black and white photographs that still blanket the far wall in my office, so many pictures across so many years of his life.

I just stared, conflicting emotions and thoughts battling for supremacy in my head. He looked back at me, smiling, then chuckling, then smiling again, just waiting. Waiting for me to be ready to know it was him.

"How..." is all I said. There was no way to ask sixty-five questions at once, so I just settled on that one. It was also disconcerting and frightening to even engage this potentially dangerous apparition in conversation, so even the one word was a struggle to get out. I had never spoken to a ghostly vision before, even one who looked as real as this one.

He laughed heartily, "How? I have no mortal idea. None whatso-ever! But isn't it just wonderful?" Ramford warmly extended his hand to help me up. After casting a suspicious eye, I took it, and stood with my deceased dad face to face.

"You're alive?" I managed to say. "Is it really... I mean, how can it really be you? And you're young again? How long have you been here?"

"I've been here about 30 minutes. Am I still alive? Ha! Yes, I haven't died yet. That's so funny to hear you ask that, but I under-stand why you would. I should ask you if you've been born yet, since I have no children. But I know you're my son-to-be." He grabbed me around the shoulder and shook me a bit, and it comforted me. "This is either some kind of time travel situation, or I'm really dreaming a bigger whopper this time than flying funnels." I said, puzzled.

"Oh yes! Time travel to be sure. It's the year of our Lord 1888 for me. What year is it for you?"

"2000..." my voice trailed off. I was believing it. Somehow, my father, Ramford Url, had met me from the year 1888 in this tunnel, where I joined him from the year 2000.

"We came through a hole in our cellar, in our house... you left a message for us!" I stammered.

"I'm sure I will, but I haven't done so yet." Ramford corrected. "My hole was a bit more exciting, if you can believe that. Darwin and I were walking on water in the North Atlantic, on a floor provided by roots, and our "hole" opened up in the sea, and down we tramped, not a half hour ago," my father explained. "And here's a further point to confuse you: whoever your mother is, I've never met her. You and I need to talk about her in detail later, when we have more time! I could use your help in finding her!" Ramford raised his eyebrows, watching my reaction to that remark, seeing how much of this I was digesting.

When I said nothing, he continued, "It doesn't take long to figure it all out. I've been here with Darwin for about a half hour. Linky's just arrived, and he's already having a ball. Come on in here and be with us," he suggested kindly, taking my arm and waiting for me to agree by moving in that direction. "I explained what I knew to Linky, and he seemed to understand without a wit of astonishment. It's not so difficult once you think about it." I followed him through the door in the wall, which, apparently had been there all along, and I hadn't seen it because it my furious ride stopped a little bit after it.

Inside the doorway the world completely changed again. My eyes filled with the sight of a cavernous room, translucent suggestions of furniture and carpeting and coffee tables and walls and doors and windows scattered everywhere. My first impression was of a large sitting room, or a very posh hotel lobby, decorated with items only half-physical, and I spotted Linky right away, lounging on a see-through sofa, sipping some sort of pink liquid from a see-through straw stuck into a see-through pineapple. I gazed around, noticing that only one other person was in the room, a very old gentleman with a very long beard who looked somewhat familiar. Not see-through, but real, like the rest of us.

"Uncle Url! I told you so!" Linky called out when he saw me, waving, "Look, just think about something and it happens! Watch this!"

As I gaped at the scene, Linky waved his hand over toward the floor in front of the half-visible fireplace, and a full-grown see-through elephant appeared, complete and alive in every detail. Even its hide was gray (in a transparent kind of way) covered with tiny brown stubbly hairs. It raised it's trunk, bared its bold tusks of ivory and roared in a deep screech that startled everyone.

"Wanna see it stand on one foot?" Linky asked me, nearly giggling at my predicament.

"Don't scare your poor Uncle to death, Linky" Ramford scolded with a smile. "Perhaps my son's aging heart can't take the stress." Ramford walked over to one of the chairs and gestured to it.

"Come on, son," he said, "have a seat and let's talk about what's going on, and why we're all here. Everything we could possibly want to know is right here in this room. And we best get started," he sat down in an adjacent chair, "because we don't have an eternity to learn it all!"

CHAPTER THIRTEEN

Aunt Purl's 1945 Packard jumped and jostled over the rough back roads, her reaction time of swerving to avoid potholes not entirely olympic class. She was en route to "The Compound", as she called it, the giant old house where the boys and Uncle Url were in dire trouble.

Frantic after this morning's phone call from Uncle Url when she learned of the attacking roots and the cryptic warnings in Ramford's journal, she immediately dashed to her faithful Packard, which was always kept waxed and fueled in the free-standing side garage. Her heartbeat soared far above it's usual level as her mind went over and over the details.

"Oh goodness, and the roots attacking poor Dinky!" she said aloud. "I've got to get the boys out of there!" and she pressed down harder on the accelerator as if to say "potholes be damned!" Still 50 minutes away from Linky and Dinky's house, a lot of dirt remained to be kicked up behind her speeding antique motorcar. ***

The ceiling fascinated me the most, and though I wanted to study the translucent objects around the room, I couldn't take my eyes off the ceiling. It seemed to extend upwards for eternity, yet something of a fog swirled around it's cavernous expanse. It seemed from instant to instant to be forming shapes, recognizable shapes, sometimes very detailed scenes of cities and crowds of people and animals, but those images would dissolve so fast I scarcely believed I saw them. Maybe I didn't, yet the fascination remained. I couldn't quite put my finger on what was going on, and it was irritating, like an itch that couldn't be isolated, but something was going on in that foggy canopy, and I had no fantasies: it knew far more about me than I did about it.

"Now son, let me introduce you to Charles Darwin. He's a very well-known Naturalist, at least to us in the 1800s!" My father said, gesturing to Darwin, who nodded in my direction in a most polite way.

"Famous! I'll say!" Linky piped up, "Charles Darwin invented Evolution, everybody knows that!"

The others looked at Linky as if he was a genius, or had spoke the most profound thing they'd ever heard. Of course, they couldn't know the future, and we, of course, took our own past for granted.

"Oh really? This must be something yet to come, Darwin? Or perhaps the future has painted you with a different brush than expected," my father remarked. "Apparently your work is known far into the next century. But for 'Evolution', not naturalism."

Darwin frowned for a moment, pondering that word. "I believe they've simply created a new word for my work. 'Origin of the Species' is the study I mostly certainly would be most remembered for, so I guess they have simply changed the verb to a noun, 'evolving' to 'evolution'. Interesting, I guess it sounded better when standing side by side with the word 'Creationism'."

Darwin turned to me directly, "Tell me, my good man. What has become of our species in the future? The year 2000, you say? A new millennium! Is it a science-based culture?"

"Ha!" I couldn't help but laugh, but my father interrupted. "Come now, we must take care of our important business first. We're not gathered in this place for trans-century chit-chat, although it would be fascinating. First we must meet our host." He paused, looking down at the floor for a moment, as if listening, but we heard nothing. "Okay, it's not time yet. We're waiting for..."

At that moment we all spun at the wailing that had suddenly commenced outside the "door" to this impossible room. Dinky, gripping Binky's hand and dragging him behind, burst into the room screaming "Uncle Url!"

They ran directly across and plowed into me, like two children desperate for adult comfort. I sat down in my chair and they climbed aboard, burying their faces in my shoulder.

"Weeee couldn't find youuuuuu!"

"You're alright..." I said gently, patting them both on the back. "You're here with Linky and I now, and, remarkably, you get to meet Grampa Url."

Dinky raised his head and looked about the group with swollen eyes. Seeing the vision of my father, his faced squinted in recognition, and then immediately buried his face again.

"A ghost!" he cried, muffled, gripping my neck tighter than before.

"No, he's real! Look!" Linky called over, jumping up to shake hands with Ramford. "See? He's not see-through like everything else, he's still alive, but in the past!" Linky paused while we all watched him, and then said with a twinkle "It's very easy to understand, dork."

Dinky pushed away from me in a start, and bolted toward Linky, fire in his eyes at the insult, the bait taken instantly, as Linky knew it would be. But instead of a collision, Dinky slid to the floor harmlessly... Linky had risen about 10 feet into the air, and slowly spun, hovering. "Whatever you imagine comes true," Linky said in a singsong fashion, making faces at us at each revolution. "You can come up here, too, if your brain is powerful enough. I doubt it."

"Just teach him how to do it," my father ordered, "and you boys don't get hurt. I'm going to get better acquainted with my son."

So we separated, with Linky and Dinky and Binky to play in the open area, while my father and Darwin and myself moved to a corner settee. When a transparent 12-foot ladder appeared and Dinky scampered up it, I knew that parity had been achieved.

"So," my father began, "please tell me how I meet your mother!" We all laughed at his joke, and it helped relieve the tension of this impossible situation.

I summoned long set aside memories: "It was at the university, she taught Literature in another section of the school. I believe you first met at some sort of teacher's conference. You never told me any of the juicy details, so I'm afraid I can't help you much beyond that. It was around 1915, as I recall."

"At a university, eh?" Ramford nodded, it made sense. "So I do end up with tenure as a professor. And what of my..."

But Darwin would have no more of the catch up: "Get organized, gentlemen!" he spoke up. "We'll not accomplish much if you jump around from ancillary anecdote to ancillary anecdote. Start at the beginning, and tell your stories as to how you got here. That's the only thing that matters right now."

He paused. "I'll begin..."

"During my travels, on the HMS Beagle and afterward, I discovered that each successive life generation was never perfect, but was different in small but substantive ways from parent to sibling. Each life form copied itself a bit differently each time, basically because of the random nature of chemical activity within the seeds. I found that over a very very long and slow process, hundreds of thousands of years, each life that gained an advantage because of something different about it born from it's parent, tended to live longer, and therefore, tended to have more offspring. Consequently, the various and subtle differences which gave that animal a life-lengthening advantage, bestowed that same trait upon it's young, which, in turn, would have life-lengthening advantages, and so forth. That's why so many animals and insect have eyesight. It's one of the amazing properties that super-extended life, because they could run and hide from predators, and see to catch food, and so forth."

"That's what's called Evolution today," I interrupted. "It changed everything. At least, for most people."

"So my theories stood the test of time? Darwin exclaimed. "Very well. But I haven't yet explained what brings me here." he shuffled in his seat impatiently. (I glanced over to see that Linky and Binky were now each floating in giant bubbles, bouncing into each other like bumper cars. Off to the side, a huge transparent hamster wheel was spinning on it's own, and Dinky was rolling within it, spinning around in what looked like an astronaut training device. All was well.)

Darwin took a deep breath and continued: "Through much study and experimentation, I later learned that even though all species have been slowly evolving over the eons and getting better into the future, by tracing their origins back to the far distant past, I discovered a remarkable thing: something gave them a jumpstart. That's the only way I can explain it. Something unprecedented happened a long time ago which gave all lifeforms a monumental leap forward. It's quite clear in the fossil records, because thirty thousand years ago we have ignorant cave dwellers, hunters and gatherers, and then almost on the exact same geological plane we have evidence of highly intelligent beings, and clear evidence of language. Drawings in linear shapes like sentences, hieroglyphics and so forth."

"Well," Ramford said, "they evolved in the brains, too, right?"

"Wrong!" Darwin retorted. "What I discovered is absolutely impossible. Without intervention, it could not happen that a cave-dwelling humanoid developed language, and all the social advantages that language brings, in so short of a time. Something intervened, and I think it's clear we're sitting right in the belly of it."

My father and I pondered on that for a moment, and then I remembered: "The journal! Oh yes, you fully explained it in your Journal!" I said to Ramford. "The fact that RNA and DNA cannot work to form life without the other being present, yet, neither of those complex molecules could have evolved unless the other already existed. It's a Chicken-and-Egg conundrum."

"RNA? DNA? What are you talking about? And what journal?" my father asked me.

"Well, you wrote it, it's all in there." I answered. "Pages and pages of chemical formulas and explanations. I've already told you more than I understand about it." and then it hit me: he had no idea what DNA was, because it hadn't been discovered until the 1950's, but... he had written about it in his journal before I was born... oh it was getting confusing now.

"The journal is what brought us here. It was hidden in the side panel of my roll top desk... it used to be *your* roll top desk... but that was over 80 years ago."

"I saw a roll top desk for sale in a shop in the Port of London when I was buying supplies," Ramford mused, "I wished I could have purchased it then and there."

"You will! I remember now! You told me you bought it in London and had it shipped over!" I exclaimed. Time travel was fun!

"At least we know you survive to do so, eh, Ramford?" Darwin winked, and our situation bore down on us again, having momentarily forgotten it in the clamor of conversation. "Are you finished?" Ramford asked of Darwin.

"Not quite. When I saw the roots in my garden pathway, and found the meaning of the message it spelled out -- a spot in the North Sea -- I elicited the aid of Ramford to arrange an expedition to that location, and soon after our arrival, a path of roots led us to a hole in the ocean, and here we are."

"Okay," Ramford said. "I wasn't doing much but studying biology when Darwin contacted me. That's really all that's pertinent."

"Then it's my turn," I said. "We were all in my office eating cake, talking about our hundred thousandth subscriber to our internet newsletter..." my voice trailed off as their faces told me they didn't understand.

"In the future, there's this thing called the Internet... well, forget about that. The boys and I make a living now publishing a periodical that over a hundred thousand people read twice a week." "Like a newspaper?" my father asked, puzzled.

"Sort of, but it's not about the news, it's about amusements on the world wide web... I'll have to explain all that later, it will take too much time now." I swallowed hard, changing my story to fit their lack of knowledge about the present day world.

"So we were in my office, which used to be your office, and Dinky was rolling around the floor and saw something on my Rolltop desk -- which used to be your roll top desk -- that he fingered, and a door opened on the side of the desk, and inside was your Journal. I read some it, and it talked about cave men and a rock-like object that had roots and swarmed all over the cave men and gave them language."

"Eureka!" Darwin shouted, "That's the proof! We did discover something that jumpstarted the species -- you wrote about it!" Darwin back-handed my father across his shoulder, exuberance clearly showing through his beard-frosted face. "And it is tied up with this creature who brought us here." he rubbed his eyes, "it's all starting to make sense. That's what we're here to learn, the secret of the helping hand that this beast gave our species."

Through all this spirited discovery, I glanced again over at the boys. Linky had an arm in the air, whooping and hollering, his other hand grabbing the reins of the Wooly Mammoth upon whose back he rode. Dinky and Binky were tossing dice at a translucent crap table, mounds of translucent chips piled high in front of them while a crowd of cheerleaders roared them on.

Darwin was speaking when I turned my attention back, "Ah, it must be time." I followed his gaze to the opposite corner of the room, and saw what he saw: a misty orb, solidifying before our very eyes. It floated above what appeared to be a heavy mahogany stand, resembling for all the world like a free standing globe of the earth... made of mist.

"Yes, that's it!" Darwin announced, standing. "Let's go touch it."

CHAPTER FOURTEEN

Aunt Purl's 1945 Packard skidded to a stop on the gravel driveway of "the Compound" as she slammed on the brakes. Her eyes widened, glancing about the yard thoroughly, expecting to see something horrible, like a giant net of roots swallowing the house and pulling it into the ground.

Nothing seemed amiss.

She sat very still in the car, trying to ignore the gentle creaking of the Packard as it cooled, it's steel and iron framework settling and condensing after the long drive. She heard nothing, and saw only the usual. She startled a bit at the Arch of Pink and Yellow Flowers which leaned askew at the front door of Linky and Dinky's Clubhouse, but that was quite a bit behind the house and didn't seem dangerous.

They were gone. The house was empty. She was too late.

Opening the jalopy's door, she stuck out the fireplace poker, her chosen weapon of defense, and examined the ground very closely before stepping out. Peering intently for any movement among the random grass and pine needles and small rocks, she stepped slowly toward the front door of the house, jumping back each time an insect moved across her field of vision.

The door was closed, but unlocked, and she opened it, expecting for all the world to see a maze of roots crisscrossing the interior like an overgrown jungle. When her eyes adjusted just a bit, there was none of that. Just furniture and lamps and small tables and a few rugs in various places across the wood floor.

"Url!" she called, still holding back from entering lest anything jump out at her at the sound of her voice. Silence.

Slowly she moved in, poker gripped in front of her with both hands, ready to bash anything that threatened. She crept through the living room, peeked into the kitchen "a mess!" she thought, then turned to cross to the stairs... then she saw the open cellar door.

"Why is that door open..." she pondered aloud, knowing full well it had been kept locked for years. Her heart jumped a beat as the realization of trouble sunk in. "It's all happening in the cellar!"

"Hello!" her voiced echoed down the steps and rang around the moist walls of the cellar, but her call went unanswered. She saw a flashlight lying at the bottom of the stairs, still on, though dim, and fearfully knew in an instant it had been dropped during a time of peril to one of her loved ones. Should she go down and get it? Should she rush down there to see if one of them (or all of them) were lying hurt? Should she call an ambulance? What would she say? ("There's nobody here! Hurry! Come help!")

She dashed down the stairs, snatched up the light and splayed it's weak light into the dead center of the cellar, straining to see and hear and feel and sense everything possible all at once.

Nothing. The dirt floors were undisturbed, no bodies, a few boxes, an old dinette set, some lumber.

Whatever was here -- whoever was here -- had vanished.

* * *

We watched and waited as the orb of mist settled into stillness, slowly rotating but no longer descending. Obviously, it was waiting for us.

"Why should we touch it?" I asked with exasperation, not expecting an answer, but I got one anyway.

"Because that's why we're here," Ramford stated.

"We must find out!" Darwin added, taking the lead in moving our group toward the orb, and before I could check the safety of the boys or pause long enough to get comfortable with the idea, Darwin had extended his right hand and thrust it into the mist. Immediately, as I watched, his hand jerked out again and he spun to face us.

"Of course! I knew it! We're part of it all!" his face beamed with wonder, his eyes looking skyward. "You'll see, come on!" he grabbed Ramford by the elbow and yanked him toward the orb. He obliged, and stuck his hand in too, then quickly pulled it out. He locked eyes with Darwin and they seemed to penetrate each other's mind, their expressions unable to keep up with the sensations their brains were experiencing. They were overwhelmed.

My logic kicked in: "Okay, that's two of you. I see no need for any of the rest of us to..." suddenly a long finger of mist jutted out from the orb and circled my neck like a lasso. While I watched, it dissipated, dissolved and was gone. My mind stopped, and I stood without thinking. I was blank.

Images burst into view in my mind's eye, and I saw and knew intimately the lives of thousands of people. Billions of people! I remembered their every thought, their every triumph, every agony, every doubt, every joy. It was a wondrous swirl, an overwhelming sense of belonging -- I was them, they were me, we lived together. We were one single person with billions of different feelings and experiences. In a flash I saw and felt all those moments of emotion within all the lives of everyone who had ever lived. Of discovery, of joy, of hunger, of pain. I lost limbs and climbed mountains and ate insects and was struck by lightning and burned alive and born alive and buried alive and beheaded and crowned a king and gave birth to untold children and enjoyed a gigantic feast and had a spear strike me through the heart and watched another's head cave in as I crushed it with a rock. I was every flower plucked, every fish pulled out the water into the choking sky. Incredibly I was soaring over a cliff toward tumultuous waters below and I pushed massive boulders into place on a pyramid and I played music and I invented a slingshot and I was hiding in a tree ready to pounce on a wolf and being carried on the shoulders of strong men as they cheered me and I whimpered in a corner as someone towered over me screaming in to my face and beating my legs with a stick... and yet, I was doing the screaming and I was doing the beating...

I saw a child being eaten by a wild animal, a simple jungle beast happy to have a good meal, while at the same time I was the child being eaten, not understanding the pain or the attention of the animal. I was both sides and every side and the final decision maker and every glory was mine and every mistake was my fault.

Every life was my life. I knew everything all at once, and then it was gone.

As my spinning mind cleared, like a powerful dream from which I just awoke, I noticed Ramford and Darwin, sitting with me on the floor near the Orb, holding hands in a circle, comforting each other silently while we digested the experience given us by our "host". Slowly, we began to regain our sense of self and independence, and the reason for hand-holding seemed to have passed, and we separated.

"Wow," I said softly. We all just sat there, as if rapidly coming off a really strong buzz. I knew I was getting back to normal when I had the presence of mind to look over to where the boys were. They were just standing amongst an eclectic collection of odd oversized translucent toys, staring at us.

"It's exactly like I deduced, yet ten-thousand fold more," Darwin said, his head still clearing from the visions.

"It's astonishing -- this changes everything! If everybody just knew, there would be no more war, no more evil," Ramford added, then standing. "We're now to go back and see the beginning, so we will understand our place at the end."

"What?" I asked, straining to get up off the floor too. "I thought this was nearly over, time to go back up to the house and start writing it all down or something. Nobody gave me any direction about 'going back'. I don't remember anything about 'going back'".

"Of course!" Darwin explained, "we're to go back, to the beginning, to the very start of the connection, to when the Beast launched it all." He looked back and forth from Ramford to myself, then nodded his head. "We must," he said with some authority, "and don't assume we each had identical visions. Many parts of it were similar, I'm sure, but we're each involved in specific roles --" he gestured over to where the boys were standing -- "and those three as well! They are a huge part of what's to come, they have their own journey to take."

"What journey is that?" Binky asked, stepping forward, but that's all I saw, because in the blink of an eye the boys were gone, and Darwin, Ramford and I were looking up through a root-encrusted hole at the sky.

CHAPTER FIFTEEN

There was nothing to do but climb out. We looked at each other, Darwin shrugged, and the three of us clambered up the footholds provided by the roots and stood looking around.

"This isn't what I expected would come next," Darwin said. We three middle-aged men were now peering around a vast scrub-brushed empty field. No, it was much larger than a field, it was a vast open plain without trees or big rocks or any discernable features at all. The ground was stony and filled with a carpet of sporadically growing weeds as far as the eye could see. It was like a desert where it rained periodically.

"If this is now some sort of survival contest, I think we're doomed," my father said. The wind was blowing gently, was warm and scented with that wild and raw smell of untamed nature. The air was most likely thick with pollen, as my sinuses would soon alert me.

"Be thoughtful now," Darwin told us. "Look around, use your eyes. We're here for good reason, but I'm sure we're too thick-headed to fathom it."

"Okay, okay, let's start simple," I said. "Look at the position of the sun. It's nearly overhead, indicating mid-day. And from it's angular position relative to the horizon, we can deduce..." I halted.

"Deduce what?" Ramford asked.

"Deduce that we're probably north of the equator?" I guessed.

"That's enormously helpful," my father smirked. "But there is something quite familiar about this area - and look, way over there (he pointed) is that a fence?"

We both stared to where he pointed, but Darwin said "Squint your eyes, men, we're standing on a road leading right in that direction!" he took off walking briskly down his imagined path. I saw no road, but the weeds were a bit thinner in a rutted sort of way.

So we walked toward the fence, which was probably a mile distant. At one point Darwin stooped to point out "odd" markings in the dusty dirt. "Tire tracks!" I said matter-of-factly, but that revelation was met with blank eyes by both my father and Darwin. Neither had seen an automobile, at least not at the age they were representing now. I explained it as best I could, they chuckled at the word "motorcar" until I also referred to it as a "horseless carriage". Then they got it.

We walked quite a ways. We should have used the time wisely to compare notes between the generations and years, but mostly we just panted. Eventually I was startled by Ramford yelling: "My house!" He was pointing to the roof of what looked like MY house. "This prairie must be the government land I built next to." He picked up speed, and we followed in suit. "Url, don't you remember the walks we would take out here? Jumping the fence and spending all day exploring?"

Indeed I did remember, for I took Linky and Dinky and sometimes Binky on that same adventure. The fact that it was forbidden
by plastic signs that told us NO TRESPASSING made it all the more
exciting. But neither in my younger years nor later did I ever find
anything of interest out here. I didn't know what "time" we were in
at the moment, exactly, but the house was standing and the land
looked the same, so it couldn't be too far in the past, or the future,
from when I had last left.

We gingerly crawled over the fence in the manner of old men,
careful, testing, unsure, but we all made it and walked tired but
purposely the rest of the way to the house.

It looked fine, clean and sound. I veered off the path a bit to get a
look around the house proper and yep -- there was our Secret
Clubhouse, right where it was supposed to me. I figured we were in
MY timeframe, the year 2000 or close to it. This was unsettling.
Fascinating, yes, but so fearsome I'd rather not be fascinated. Or
maybe I did. I was getting queasy. I'm about to invite my deceased
father into what used to be his house (before I inherited it) with an
additional guest, Charles Darwin, who had personally never
witnessed indoor plumbing or electrical power or temperature
conditioned air or television or -- the internet.

"I can't believe the sight of it!" My father whispered, looking at his
house in it's modernized condition. Over the years I had added rain
gutters, storm windows, outdoor lighting, a fire escape from the
third floor, a skylight and brick walkways. But I knew the real

surprise would have to wait until he saw the features of the inside. "What's that round metal disc attached to the outside of my office pointing askew at the sky?" he asked.

"Uh, DirecTV," I answered. "It's a satellite television reception system for, uh, entertainment and news and so forth."

"How does it provide entertainment? News of what? Current events?"

"Well, I'll have to show you..." we were approaching the front walk, and I stopped them.

"Listen dad, Mr. Darwin. We're about 100 years away from when you were last, uh, living. So, lots of things have changed and you might not immediately understand the technology and all that, and..."

"On with it, boy!" Darwin barked. "I'll explore the future for myself. I'll be asking you to explain when I ask you. You're no tour-guide." he stepped up the porch and stood at the front door. He gripped the handle and pulled, then pushed, then pulled again, frustrated it wouldn't open. He stepped back and turned to me.

"It must be locked," he growled.

"Well, probably not, you just have to push down on this lever here to disengage the latch." I demonstrated in slow motion, then swung open the door and leaned in. The last time I was here roots were threatening to envelope the whole house. But it seemed normal right now.

They followed me in, ooing and awing quietly over the decor, the furniture, the lamps, the "color" pictures of family and friends and so forth. My father stepped up to our TV, a nice 40" Sony in the corner. "This is where I placed my RCA Victor radio. It was about the size of this oddity. Where did it go? We need to catch up on the events of the day." He swung his head around the room quickly, then at me: "Do you have a calendar, son? We need to know the date. At least what year it is."

"Right, right, in here." I moved to the kitchen and to the side of the refrigerator where a calendar clung by magnets. "June 2000. Nothing's changed," I told them. "It's the exact same date I left to find... you guys."

"The Year 2000, my Lord!" Darwin sat himself down slowly at the kitchen table, about to faint yet curious enough to run his hand over the modern aluminum ridging of the table edge. "I can't believe it. This whole thing must be a mirage, a vision. The Beast is leading us through hallucinations!"

I mumbled something about doubting that because it was my house and my stuff and all, but my attention was turned. Ramford had opened the refrigerator. He stared at the contents, held out his hand to feel the cooling, then looked at me with marvel in his eyes. "Son, this is a wonderful wonderful invention." His voice was hushed and reverent. "No King in history has ever lived this richly. You have wealth and powers beyond those of the gods!"

"Yes, the refrigerator, it's great. We like it a lot." This wasn't turning out to be as fun as I might have imagined it would be. They were respecting and honoring mundane everyday items that I so much took for granted. I knew I would have to be gentle with them, this couldn't be easy for citizens of the 19th century.

"Hmmm, is this chocolate? A powerdized delicacy! How novel!" Darwin was licking his finger, having wiped up a bit of cake mix the boys had left splattered on the table.

"Uh, yeah, they were baking a cake earlier," I answered.

"So, cooking is still a necessity in the year 2000?" The sarcasm in Darwin's remark didn't go unnoticed.

"What's this box?" my father asked, pointing to the microwave. "Is it another entertainment contraption you spoke of?"

"Well, no, that's a microwave oven..." I walked over to it.

"An oven! Where do you put the wood?"

"It uses microwaves to heat... here, I'll show you." I drew a little water into a coffee cup and place it inside, then set it to 30 seconds.

They both jumped at the beep when the light went out. I realized neither man had ever heard an electronic tone before. "Not much flame that I can see," Darwin said.

"Here, take the cup. It's hot!" my father took it, then set it down

on the counter like it was demon possessed.

"So it's a heating box. You have a box that cools and a box that heats. And they're the devil's own, like all the other black magic in this house!" He was smiling, he knew it wasn't magic at all, but this situation allowed me to use a great saying from Arthur C. Clark: "Any sufficiently advanced technology is indistinguishable from magic," I quoted.

"'Tis true, 'tis true," Darwin commented, nodding.

I let them explore for awhile. The incredible journey we were on would have to wait until the roots showed themselves or their intentions or whatever was about to happen next in this odyssey. But for now, I followed them around the house as they touched and smelt and lifted their eyeglasses to get a closer look at what I thought was just regular stuff. They didn't know the TV could be turned on, and I steered them away from it for now. That would take an entire day to demonstrate adequately, and it would reveal the world as it is in this century, and I didn't want them diverted off course by MTV just yet. At this point, the wrong music video might just be enough to bring on a stroke.

They laughed and laughed in the bathrooms. They must have flushed the toilet at least a dozen times. They removed the lid, investigated the inner workings of the tank. "A buoyant ball used as a leveling device and simultaneously as a terminating interchange! Brilliant!" and so forth. The exclamations went on and on. The shower head was loose anyway, so the two scientists quickly figured out how to unscrew it and couldn't contain their glee, "It divides the stream into multiple streamlets that not only provides wider coverage but more pressure! That sure beats an old maiden pouring a bucket of ice cold well-water over our heads, eh old man?!"

Within the space of half an hour, my father and his new buddy in crime, Charles Darwin, were exposed to the incredible inventions of the last 120 years. The light bulb, refrigerant, pressurized pipes, airplanes and the space shuttle (Linky had some Testor models hanging from his ceiling), plastic in every sort of shape and color, radios using the transistor to make them small, digital clocks, fancy typography, the iPod, color printing (I turned beet red when my father picked up a copy of Maxim magazine in Dinky's room. He didn't know how to leaf through it and fumbled badly at the pages and gave it up when Darwin called him over to examine Dinky's Christmas Tree of AOL discs. I slid the magazine in a drawer.)

They were exhausted by the time we reached my office (or was it now my father's office again?). I had my answer when he said to Darwin "Look here, my office. Come in for a spell and rest a bit, old chum."

They sauntered in like they owned the place, eyes scanning for something new to misunderstand. But when my father saw his roll top desk, his hands flew wide open, "That's the desk I saw in London! At one of the shops near the port! I wanted to buy it then and there but couldn't..." he turned slowly to me. "This desk, where did you get?"

"I inherited it from you, dad. It's my most prized possession."

He walked over and sat down, running his fingers along its edges, slowly closing the roll top, then opening it again, enjoying the precision and ease of movement. "It's beautiful. Just beautiful. I guess this means I sent for it sometime in the future. Well, sometime in my future, that is."

He didn't even notice my laptop sitting right there in plain view, thank goodness it was closed. They'd dearly love to see a keyboard and play with it as the letters appeared magically in direct succession on the glowing glass panel (*I'm talking like them now!*) but that could wait until later.

"Did you know about this?" Without thinking I pointed to the side of the desk where Dinky had found the hidden compartment. But - - maybe I shouldn't show him the hiding spot. Maybe he wasn't yet supposed to know yet. And the book! His journal! Should I give it to him now, before he's even written it?

Too late. He was off the chair and on his hands and knees studying the hidden chamber inside the desk's side panel. "Very interesting! No, I didn't know about it. You must have found something that the original owner knew, or had fashioned by a skilled carpenter." He lifted his old-fashioned glasses to his forehead and worked the door and hinges. "Such fine work! When it's closed, it's invisible to the unaided eye." He sat back on his haunches and asked me, "So, it was empty?"

The moment of truth. Should I tell him about the Journal? It contained an enormous amount of information about his future, my past, that weird beast thing, the roots, how it came to be, and all those formulas about DNA he couldn't possible know in his time. These thoughts and all the disastrous time-travel paradoxes from every Star Trek episode I had ever seen flooded my brain. If he ever went back to the past, to his own time, he'd have knowledge of the future (important, vital knowledge of the future) that couldn't help but alter the timeline, the life he would lead, the work he would accomplish.

What would Picard do?

"Ah, I can see from your face it *did* contain something. Something you're afraid to share with me," he said. "Alright, maybe you're right. Maybe I shouldn't know what it is."

Darwin settled everything: "Hogwash! Give the man what you found, Url. This is exactly why we're here! Do you think porcelain flushing chairs is why the Beast brought us through time? No! It's for you to present to Ramford, and probably me too, whatever it is you have that we didn't! So go get it, and be quick about it!"

"It's in the top left drawer of my desk, er, your desk."

Ramford quickly stood and whipped open the drawer, removing his leatherbound journal. He look puzzled at the embossed numbers on the cover, then started flipping. "This is queer," he said. "This is certainly my handwriting, yet I swear I've never written any of it." He flipped through a few more pages, slowing down to read more and more. "This can't be...." he voice trailed off.

"Well, what have you, Ramford?" Darwin asked, a bit more agitated than before.

"It's as if..."

"Yes? Yes?"

My father cleared his throat. "It seems to me that this contains my narrative of this very journey we are on now, and apparently it's conclusion. It starts before we began our sea voyage, and seems to run well beyond it. Yet, I never wrote about our sea voyage. Very curious....and something which should be of great interest to you, Darwin."

Darwin's pointy eyebrow lifted.

"Something called DeoxyriboNucleic Acid. I've abbreviated it here as 'DNA'."

"What in blazes is it?" Darwin asked.

"Some kind of code naturally, deliberately, embedded within every cell, instructing it how to form, what type of creature to fashion and the characteristics it will have as an adult," he frowned and read some more. "and it controls every living thing, from the smallest to the mightiest," He looked up at Darwin.

"Ha! I knew it!" Darwin exclaimed. He started to rise from the recliner to perhaps dance a little jig, but thought better of it and settled back.

"Url, tell me, boy. Is this DNA something you know of? Is it known in the Year 2000?"

"Yes, of course, sure. They teach it in the schools. I think I have a book about it here somewhere..." I started a search of my bookshelves, tilting my head hard over to better read the titles.

"Is it a mature science? By that I mean, has it been fully decoded and..."

"Yes, they know all about it," I interrupted. "Here's a book on it." I handed Darwin the volume, who startled at the colorful picture on the cover. "They call that a 'double helix'," I explained. "It's what DNA is supposed to look like, or something, I really don't know that much."

They both wanted to read, so I left them there while promising to return shortly, and scurried down to the door under the stairs. The key was, remarkably, still in my pocket even after all we'd been through. I opened it up, stuck my head in to -- what? "listen" for danger? I grabbed the flashlight still laying on the floor where Dinky dropped it and headed down, using the beam as a sword to slice up the darkness and show me those roots and that hole. But it was gone. I was surprised and stymied and fearful all at once. No hole meant no way to get back to the last place where I last saw Linky and Dinky and Binky. And where were they now, anyway?

I was worried about them. So far nobody had been hurt during all this, so I was hopeful that the intention of the roots was pure and kind and wholesome.

But I was good at fooling myself.

CHAPTER SIXTEEN

It wasn't until I re-locked the cellar door and turned did I see Aunt Purl's note lying on the table by the couch. My heart started pounding in my chest as I read it:

"Dear Url, I can't find you anywhere! I fear the worst. I went to get the sheriff. I truly hope you are OK and will read this note!"

The sheriff! Oh no! That meant deputies and radios and the press and a whole bunch of hoopla and prying eyes and questions that we do not need right now! We're in the middle of an investigation that has something fantastic at the conclusion of it and nobody is going to understand my time-traveling father and his partner. And what of the boys? I can't produce them, I don't know where they are or when they're coming back -- why haven't I reported them missing? Will the forensic staff search the grounds of our compound for freshly turned dirt? Oh no-sir-re-bob, we do not need any help from the police or anybody else right now. This has to play it's way out in private. The roots and the holes might be gone for the moment, but those two older gentleman in circa 1880 attire (with who knows what kind of old-fashioned identification or paperwork in their pockets) will not know how to handle today's police. This is a nightmare!

I bolted up the stairs two at a time and rushed into my office. A paper airplane flew past my face, apparently the same paper airplane left on one of the bookshelves by Dinky. The elderly scientists had figured out how to toss it. "What is this flying notebook paper, son? Did you know it could sail unaided if propelled in..."

"Yes, yes, of course. It's just a paper airplane." I reached down to grab Darwin by the shoulder. He was relaxing in my old recliner, and was loving the foot rest. "Come on! We've got to get out of here now! Aunt Purl has gone and summoned the police because she couldn't find us. They'll be here any second..."

"Ah, young Purl. A fine lady she must be now," my father started but I hushed him with a flat hand jutted in his direction. "Listen!" I whispered.

The unmistakable sound of tires-on-gravel rumbled outside, coming from the front of the house. The cops were here!

"I don't know that word 'police'," my father stated. "Are they friend or foe?"

"Usually friends -- in this case, FOES!" I was exasperated trying to push them out the door and down the hall. Both men were holding tight to their respective books. For lack of better reasoning, I assumed that's what the beast wanted, for them to see the future and come into possession of those books. But for now, the police were the urgent matter: "They'll be asking a ton of questions, and they won't take 'time travel' for an answer. So move it!"

Darwin shuffled faster and led the way down the hall as fast as holding both handrails would allow. We reached the bottom and I steered them toward the cellar door as the first knock rapped on the front door.

I fumbled and nearly broke the key getting it back into the cellar door lock, but finally twisted it and pulled it open. "In! IN!" The two elderly scientists obediently slid into the darkness. I pulled the door closed behind me.

Feeling around the top stair landing I found the flashlight and clicked it on. "A flameless torch! Intriguing!" one of them said.

"Never mind, down the steps," I pointed the way with the flash-light beam. "I'll wait here. I don't think these old wooden planks will hold the weight of the three of us."

Darwin led again, with my father on his tail. I tried to point the flashlight around their shoulders so they could see the steps, and the splashing of the light seemed to help. I waited until they had reached the bottom before starting down myself...

At this point, reality flip-flopped. That is to say, I knew full well I was sneaking down the cellar stairs to join my father and his friend, Charles Darwin, in an attempt to hide from the police who were coming in the front door to "help" us. But on the other hand, that scenario flip-flopped with another completely different reality. My last footstep onto the cellar floor didn't hit the dirt, it landed on a bed of roots -- a moving, swirling, coiled rope of roots -- that started snaking their way up my body, encasing my legs, my torso and finishing off with my arms. In the space of a few seconds I was immobilized, wrapped in roots like mummy. Smaller thread-like roots started circling my neck and quickly wrapped around my whole head, leaving two polite holes for my eyes, my nose and mouth.

Now, I don't want to disrupt the pace and flow of this story, but you must realize that had my whole self been suddenly (and rapidly) entwined by roots a week ago, I'd probably pass out, or worse, have a heart attack. But we humans, we sure do get used to things quickly, and I was in the right mindset to be rootbound. I didn't even vomit. It was a surprise, of course, but not a big one.

The roots gave me enough play to turn my head, and just as I suspected, the funnel-shaped hole of roots had returned to the center of my cellar. It led down into deep darkness, but this time, I knew where it went.

As I watched, I saw my father and Darwin hobble over to it, hands on hips. They took a long look at it, like two old men standing in the yard over a lawnmower that wouldn't start. Darwin bent down and pointed to something in the roots, Ramford stooped to see it closer, then both men stood up laughing. Darwin gestured toward the hole as if say "after you", and my father promptly complied. And then both men vanished into the darkness without so much as a wave goodbye to me.

I've had a some time to think about what happened next, and this is for certain the most difficult part of the story to tell, primarily because there's no evidence, nothing hard and fast and solid to show you. The odyssey we went through is all over now, but when

I sit back in my chair, stocking feet up on the roll top desk, I wonder about my father and Charles Darwin, even though they're always alive way back in their own time. I can't reach through 80 years of time to speak with them again, but maybe that's for the better. In any event, it's the way nature wants it.

You're wondering what happened to Linky & Dinky & Binky, aren't you? Well them I don't miss -- I see them and talk to them every day even though they're not here, but first let me try to remember everything I can about the return of my father and Charles Darwin back to their own time...

While I was wrapped up in roots, I began to see images. The roots were oozing sights and sounds, like a dream, like a lucid dream, directly into my skull. Hazy at first, and then more clearly, I saw my father and Darwin climb out of a hole in the sea, the same hole built from strong thick-knitted roots. They scrambled up, both with their respective books locked tightly under their arms, and started back toward the ship. The pictures sped up in my mind as I watched them climb aboard, hide the books in their cabins and intermingle with the crew. Very quickly they had returned to London, and I smiled as I witnessed Ramford dicker over the price of that roll top desk in the old tyme Mercantile store fronting the docks in England. Some time later, I can't tell how long, he's on a ship back to America, accompanied by Darwin, with the giant desk boxed up in the hold of the passenger vessel. He checked on it daily during that three week voyage.

I watched in dawning amazement as my house began construction -- craftsmen of the 19th century building with wood and brick this very same old three-story colonial. Ramford was on the scene every day, sometimes looking at the sky before pointing out some-thing on the blueprints -- was he remembering how this house looked today, and trying to duplicate it? One odd scene showed my father in the house much later, as a very old man, apparently in "our" office on the third floor, kneeling and doing something to the right side of the roll top desk. The Journal had been found in the left side of the desk -- was he putting a secret compartment in the right side? We never checked the right side!

The moving images flashed to Charles Darwin, studying in a cozy chair which had been amended with a make-shift foot rest. Apparently he was also bringing knowledge of the 21st century back to his time! I saw him giving lectures, attending many meet-ings in small rooms which, for some reason, I took to be government buildings. He was collaborating with powerful officials -- probably government scientists -- revealing the future? His new-found knowledge of biology? I couldn't tell, but I worried about that.

"Hi Uncle Url! My, what an empty head you have." It was Linky's voice! I looked around again, the roots loosening even more, starting to unravel now and fall off. Linky wasn't anywhere, but then again, I didn't hear him so much as "think" him.

"Bet you can't find us!" now Dinky's voice -- but he was nowhere to be seen. Binky immediately chimed in with "you're not going to believe all the cool free stuff I found, I know everything and every-where to get it, at little or no cost!" It sure sounded like Binky, but as I stepped out of the remaining swirl of roots I realized they were all communicating telepathically. At least, that's what the voices in my head led me to believe.

I called out into musty air of the lonely cellar, noticing as I did that the root's hole had vanished, again.

"Boys! Where are you? *How* are you? Where have you been?" I wanted to know everything as quickly as possible -- and I did. I heard Linky's voice distantly calling "Watch this, Uncle Urllllll" but the words faded away as huge flashing pictures filled my eyes as if I were hovering right in the middle of a fireworks display. I saw the beast under the ground, I saw staccato images from history as roots would appear, hug a person's foot, then slither away and I knew something monumental had happened. Lincoln, Washington, Da Vinci, Copernicus, multiple Popes, merchants, kings, soldiers, generals, a young girl I gathered was Joan of Arc-- all different types of people, most of which I didn't recognize by sight but I knew them to be history-makers -- they were all influenced by the roots. I saw thousands of robed and bearded men, crouched and writing on scrolls or papyrus with long pens, all sitting on or in someway being touched by a root.

The roots were everywhere but always hidden. They pushed an iceberg into Titantic's path, they were highly active in the forests and woods, maneuvering to keep certain cavemen alive while others they let die. They caused an apple to fall on Newton's head, the roots provided the nail to be found for Martin Luther to hammer the papers on the church door. While watching more than I could understand or fathom, I came to know that the roots were controlling everything, but not as a power-hungry being, it was building something. Building a civilization, pulling the strings, moving the pieces around in a long-lasting concerted effort to bring about the conditions of today.

And then I saw the boys. Alive, happy... and busy! They were floating in a soup of roots, gesturing, nodding, talking. They were in charge of something, running an organization, making decisions, yet laughing, moving jokes around (moving jokes around?). It's hard to describe.

But they weren't the only ones! By golly, that was Einstein in there! I recognized him straightaway. He was deep in a pile of numbers and symbols and vibrating marble-like orbs (molecules? quantum stuff?). He, too, was in charge of something, making decisions, manipulating knowledge and dolling out scientific discoveries in rapid fashion. For an instant I saw other old bearded men, obviously great scientists of old, still working, factoring, inventing.

What the heck was I seeing? -- that was Mother Theresa! I recognized her too! She was healing, consoling, bringing peace and comfort. She was working in conjunction with... Albert Schweitzer? Sun Tzu was conferring with Winston Churchill -- who was that with them? Patton? Eisenhower? Rommel? This was all too much to believe, or understand.

"Url..." someone said gently. I waited for more, not sure I heard anything in the first place. "Do you understand now?" It was Ramford, my father. His image formed in front of me as clouds dissipated.

"Understand? Well, I understand that I'm insane."

"No son, you're not insane. It all makes perfect sense. You have all the pieces to this puzzle, you just need to assemble them."

"Can you help me?" I had already been talking to myself the last ten minutes, so I might as well continue.

"The Beast is actually from another place. It, and others like it, move throughout the universe, finding planets where the seed of life has begun, and it helps them. It accelerates their development. It gives them language, then a strong sense of family, then communities and laws, instruction on how to find food and build shelters. It eventually brings them technology, and understanding of their world. Medicine, education, advanced communication, all the things you enjoy today."

The last word drifted off. I could tell he wasn't finished, he was waiting for me to catch up.

"Yes, that seems apparent now, from your Journal and how it brought us together... but what of Linky and Dinky and Binky? What of Darwin? How to do they fit into all this? How do I fit into all this?"

I could hear the smile in his voice, "We're passing through a transition now, a passage into another level of civilization. Soon the world will be connected and as one like it never has been before. A worldwide community brings with it peace and understanding between the parts."

He paused quite a while, then he said "the internet."

Oh! Oh my! Well, that's a big thing, sure is. The beast is bringing us the internet, or at least the technology for it. I was beginning to understand.

"So that's where the boys come in? To help with the internet?" I asked.

"Much more than that, actually, they have become the internet. What you know now as the World Wide Web will very soon, very quickly, become the very thing that connects each person on the planet with each other. It will supply the telephone, the television, the radio, the library, the schoolhouse, newspapers, music. In a few short years you'll laugh at having needed to go to school, for learning will be automatic -- through the internet. Communication with anyone -- anywhere -- will be instanteous. It's a brave new world that's coming, and it's bringing peace and prosperity with it. Entertainment designed and customized specifically for each person will be free and plentiful. Through the help of the Beast, wars will vanish. With the help of Einstein and the Beast fantastic new engines and sources of power will make energy as free and plentiful as oxygen. Many other vast improvements will be made on Earth before the joining with others in the universe -- but the part about the internet, that's the job of Linky and Dinky and Binky. They are the ones who are going to bring it all to the world, with the help of the Beast. It's a glorious privilege."

I stammered "They are the ones who will bring it all to the world... what? when? Aren't they coming back?"

"They never left, nor will they ever leave again. You'll always be in contact with them, through the internet. They have a magnificent purpose, and they have already begun carrying it out."

"What do they think of this? Can I speak with them?" I was only three-quarters sure I was speaking to my father, this might be an impersonator, a ruse.

"Sure, just speak!" my father replied.

"Linky! Can you hear me?"

"No need to shout, Uncle Url, I'm right here," the voice of Linky answered.

"Okay, just for identification, if you're really Linky, tell me what you and Dinky did to Binky on the last April Fool's Day."

"We scribbled brown magic marker in his white underpants." True. It was Linky.

"Okay Linky, did you hear what Grampa Ramford told me?"

"Yes, of course, he's 100% right -- we're fine, we're busy, and we're having a blast!"

Dinky and Binky piped in, too, so I was convinced.

"Can you never come back? Come back the way you used to be, in a body and so forth?"

"SURE!"

I spun around, and there he was, large as life. I reached to hug him but my arms swang around thin air.

"Oops! Over here! You're too slow, Uncle Url!" Linky called, laughing.

I turned to see him now behind me.

"Okay, joker, nice trick. Now let me have a proper hug."

And that was that. It wasn't a bad situation, since the boys had the chance to help the Beast make the world a better place, and I eventually learned that Darwin's job with the Beast was to influence and aid scientists on earth as they developed genetic engineering and bio-medicines. Since nanotechnologies also required genetic coding, he was (is) responsible for that, too. He couldn't have been happier.

My father, he's a writer at heart, so he's finishing what he started: The Greatest Story in the Universe. He's following the events of the Beast and others as they unfold, documenting the entire affair. People will be fascinated to one day learn how events turned not on chance, but on the influence of the Beast. It's going to be a helluva best seller in about a century or two!

Maybe he'll title it 'Roots'.

Nah.

* * *

Aunt Purl was the only one in the driveway. As it turns out, the police wouldn't lift a finger until 24 hours had passed, so we never really had to worry about them at all. It took some time, and quite a few cups of tea, but I eventually told Aunt Purl the whole story. She was terrified to learn that the vast expanse of government land next to our house was where one of the Beast's nodules resided deep underground, but I reminded her it had only bothered us once in a 100 years, so it should remain peaceful for another 100 years.

I still run Linky & Dinky Enterprises, of course, still from my third floor office, still from the roll top desk. The boys do write the newsletter, as it is an important part of their bringing the internet to it's full spectacular glory. You can watch their progress. It was only a couple of years ago that wireless internet was impossible. Now it's commonplace. Before you know it, the internet will grow to encompass our entire lives, the best tool mankind ever made (with a little help from you-know-who). Linky & Dinky are intrically involved in that, so stay in touch with them through our web site and e-mail newsletters.

I happen to know a few secrets about the future and Linky & Dinky, but I've dare not reveal more just now -- but stay tuned, stay subscribed to Linky & Dinky -- it's going to be a great ride!

Submitted faithfully,
Uncle Url

PS: What about that vision I had of my father putting something into the right hand side of my roll top? -- an act he must have performed some 80 years in the past? Well I investigated, of course.

The right side of the desk *did* conceal a secret compartment identical to the one we found on the left hand side. Propped within it was another journal of my father's, this one titled: *The Others*. Under the front cover was a handwritten note to me, which I have permission to share with you...

My dearest son,

I finally met your mother! A great sadness in my life is that she left us so early, but not before bringing you into our lives. In my time (today), you are only a young man, 12 years old. You're bright and honest and of good character. I am enormously proud of you. I haven't, I couldn't, tell your younger self what is to come. Part of the strength and wisdom you have in later years is due to all the events of the future which will combine to mold you into the great man you are in your time. I shan't corrupt that.

I never knew Linky or Dinky or Binky in my time, but during our "adventure" I saw in them wonderful attributes, instilled in their souls no doubt by you. I look forward to my life in the hereafter with the Beast, I intend to work with all my family closely. And eventually, you.

I realize as I write this some eighty years will pass until you read it (and the journal), but the book's accuracy should stand the test of time. It's the story of where the Beast came from, its magnificent home planet. After I returned from your time, the Beast taught me more about how it runs our world, and countless other worlds, and untold trillions of other civilizations throughout our infinite Universe. You and I didn't have time to discuss if men of the 21st Century were aware of life off-planet, but I give you that knowledge in this account.

You may share this note as you see fit, but not my book The Others --
*that's for an even later time, when the boys and all the others have
finished shaping mankind into the glorious force it will become.*

*Farewell son! I love you and Purl and those rapscallions too. All
things end, as must this message.*

Until we meet again, in trust

Ramford

*Postscript: I borrowed a paper portrait from you, it's in the back of the
book.*

And so it was, a faded 4x6 color photograph of myself and Aunt
Purl with the three boys, taken just a few weeks ago during Easter.
The last time I saw it, it was attached to our refrigerator by a
magnet. Apparently he pocketed it when he was here, and kept it
for the rest of his life. That pleased me a great deal.

I put it back on the refrigerator door.

Uncle Url's
Middle-Aged Magic!

If old people are so smart, then why are they always getting ripped off by telemarketers and scammers? Well, I supposed it's because we're *not* all the same, just like all newborn babies are *not* cute.

But we (the older) know stuff! Sure we do, as do you. Learning takes place in a linear fashion, one new tidbit after the other. So on the timeline of life, those closer to the right-hand edge have *probably* acquired more information than those just starting out (I'm not telling you anything you don't already know -- yet).

... so, when I said "crucial" facts of life, keep in mind that not every one of these juicy nodules of knowledge will tickle your fancy, but I'm betting a bunch of them will. If so, I'm happy.

The criteria I used when picking my brain was to choose only those revelations which surprised me when I learned them. I figured that way I'd have a shot at surprising you, too.

Let's see what the old man came up with >>

After slathering BBQ sauce all over the chicken, the back yard barbecue grill is in a terrible mess. No problem! Let it cool, then lay the grate (just the grate, not the entire grill) into the lawn grass for one or two days. Voila! Nature will clean it for you. Bugs, microbes and who-knows-what-all will munch every bit of mess off it. Rinse the grill for next time - - the intense heat of the flame will de-germ it quite adequately.

When you see the traffic light turn red, take your foot off the gas. Coast up to it! Why hurry up and wait? Do this as a habit, you'll save a ton of money on gas over time.

Here's something I used to do years and years ago. In my 20's, I was always having to get up early for work or school, and I just hated dragging myself out of bed. So what I did was keep a glass of water and half of a No-Doz caffeine pill on my nightstand. When the alarm rang, I didn't bother with the snooze button, instead I swallowed the No-Doz and *instantly* (and I mean *immediately*) I was wide awake and ready to go. Be careful of adding coffee to this trick, because it might make your heart beat too fast. Skip the coffee or skip the pill. Caffeine is cumulative and you do not develop immunities to it.

I truly see no point to catching grass clippings. The bags are heavy, they slow you down, they're messy to empty into plastic bags -- just forget 'em! Let the cut grass fly. It lands amid the standing grass and converts to nice nutritional mulchiness, and it's invisible. So why bother?

For Gosh sakes, change your own oil! It will cost you about $8.00 instead of $35 to $45 to have JiffyDude do it. It's quite easy on most cars, all you need is something to lift the car up about 6 to 8 inches. Use a drive-up ramp or any kind of jack, the simpler/easier the better. Your car's Owner's Manual will instruct you on lifting the car, and where the oil filter and oil drain are. Drain the oil, unscrew the old oil filter (always ALWAYS replace the oil filter when changing oil) install the new filter (takes 30 seconds) and then pour the proper amount of oil in. It's fun, and you'll beat the 10 minutes JiffyDude never can. Also, if you change the oil every 2,000 instead of ever 3,000 you'll get a whole lot better performance and many additional *years* of trouble-free use from the car.

Bottled Water -- I always buy Distilled. Distilled Water is formed from cooled steam, meaning nothing at all (except minerals) can be in it. Viruses and bacteria and foul smells cannot transport through the steam. It's the cleanest water there is, and tastes the very best of all the over-hyped other filtered waters. Don't be scared off by the word "distilled", it just means SUPER PURE, and TASTY!

Men are supposed to take at least 81 mg. of aspirin every day, to thin the blood just a little bit and help prevent heart attacks. Get St. Joseph's Chewable aspirin in the 81 mg. size. Keep the bottle in your desk or near your computer, it's a lot quicker and easier to pop a chewable every day rather than having to keep water handy.

I don't recommend buying DVDs as a rule, since you'll rarely watch them a 2nd time, and if you want to -- rent it! And it will be on Cable TV soon enough. Also, if you *do* buy DVDs, you can usually always find *full screen* versions to match your TV, but you have to order them thru www.amazon.com

When filling up with gas, turn off the switch at the pump and then squeeze the nozzle again -- up to 8 ounces more of fuel will dispense from the pressure inside the hose. Do that every time and you get a free tank of gas every few years.

If you've been waiting to buy a digital camera, don't wait any longer! The "exposed" pictures store on the camera until you attach a wire and download them to your computer. It's effortless. Every picture you take digitally is free! You can shoot hundreds, store them on your computer, burn CDs or DVDs galore. No buying film, no developing costs or waiting to "see how the pictures came out". Buy the most megapixel you can afford, because that makes cropping and enlargements crystal clear.

You'll never get a second chance to take a photograph or video of your children. You've heard it before, but it's 100% true: they grow up so fast. You'll be thrilled to have their childhood on film after they move out. Take all you can, document everything, you'll enjoy them often the rest of your life.

Call your credit card company and request a lower interest rate. If you've been making payments on time, they'll likely cut your rate by 20% or more, but they won't do *anything* unless you ask. I've done this myself, it worked on both my credit cards. And boy did I feel smart afterwards! Of course, you shouldn't carry a balance, but as a self-employed old guy, I carry a little bit so I can continue to have a credit history of making payments on time. If you're beyond the Career Years, credit isn't as easy to get as it was when you were young, so take care of it.

Get yourself to Graceland before you die. It's one of the truly inspirational and fascinating museums and tourist traps in the country. Elvis Presley's (small but palatial) home in Memphis, Tennessee has been restored to the way it was when Priscilla lived there with Elvis. Once you walk the Wall of Fame and see the 1000s of trophies, gold records and other awards given to Elvis, you'll understand why they say: "If you're an Elvis fan, no explanation is necessary. If you're not an Elvis fan, no explanation is possible." They also say "50 Million Elvis Fans Can't Be Wrong." I don't think we are.

Get into the 21st Century and use eBay. You can almost always find a big selection of just what you're looking for, and you'll never find it cheaper than on eBay. I've been using eBay to build a collection of my favorite series of short stories (Ellery Queen Mystery Magazine and its wonderful sister publication, Alfred Hitchcock Mystery Magazine). I buy them in big lots of 20 or 30 so I can eventually own every one of these magazines ever published, and the duplicates aren't wasted -- I package them together and sell them back to other collectors on eBay!

(Related to the above) Read short stories. Books require a long term commitment and an expansive attention span. Short stories are quick, spunky, clever, fast-paced with twisty endings. Of course, I recommend Ellery Queen or Alfred Hitchcock mysteries for their incredibly wide range of topics and locales (and the butler never does it). Very clever, I like them a lot.

When it's chilly outside, there's no need to heat the whole house if you're going to be spending most of the evening in a single room watching TV or reading. Instead, get an electric blanket (a heating blanket that gets warm when you plug it in), and lay it down on your easy chair. Sit upon it, warm and cozy. Heat rises, so it's very efficient in dispersal. It costs far less in power than a space heater, and hours of use really make an impact (for the better) on your electric bill. Wal-Mart has electric blankets for about $20.

Rechargeable batteries are the bomb! When you use the same set of batteries in your MP3 player or radio 100 times, the savings become clear, don't they? And no running to the store to spend $2 per battery every so often. They say that worrying about batteries is the mark of Middle Age. Maybe so. I do know the batteries are the most shoplifted item by senior citizens, so maybe there's some truth to that.

Don't ever ever ever buy the Extended Warranty on any item you purchase ever ever ever! The only reason stores are selling you the warranty (and they get pushy about it sometimes, don't they?) is because *they know you'll never use it*! Oftentimes, sales clerks earn a bonus of up to 50% of the cost of the warranty, because it's all free money. You'll lose the paperwork, it won't cover the specific problem you are having, or it will expire before the item breaks. If something doesn't break within the first 90 days (when you can return it for a refund or replacement anyway) then the odds are it will last a long long time.

If you're shopping for a new computer, I heartily recommend Macintosh. They are easy. They don't break. They update software automatically over the internet. They have Help files all over the place. Once you learn how to use one program, you've learned them all. Put a dent in the Universe, use a Macintosh.

Over-the-counter nasal decongestant sprays are addictive because the more you use them, the more you *must* use them. That's great for the manufacturer because you must keep buying the sprays! What nasal sprays do is temporarily shrink nasal membranes and passages so you can breath easier... but when the chemical wears off, the membranes expand again, only this time a little bit weaker. Over a short time they get *very* weak and it will take more more spray to shrink them. So use something (a pill, not a spray) with pseudoephedrine in it. It's the only one on the market, it's the only thing that works without side effects. Eyedrops are the same way, Visine is a vasal constrictor which shrinks the blood vessels in your eyes to reduce bloodshotness. When it wears off, they enlarge again... but blood vessels are now a bit weaker so your eyes are a bit redder. Use an eye drop antihistime instead, like Naphcon-A or Clear Eyes.

Those little black AC/DC converters that power everything from your telephone to your modem are *always* pulling power from the wall whether you are using the product or not. It's like the gizmo is always turned on, as far as electrical usage goes. Unplug them when not in use to save energy.

Replace your 75 Watt and 100 Watt light bulbs with incandescent bulbs (the type that spiral like neon tubes). You can get them at home improvement stores. They use only 5% of the same electricity and provide just as much light that the old-fashioned energy-hog bulbs do, as long as you use a higher wattage. For example, to adequately replace a regular 75 Watt bulb, use a "100 Watt Compatible" incandescent bulb instead. And no heat! They generate no heat all -- you can place your hand directly on them.

If you're buying a stove, get the kind they call "countertop", where only the area around the burners gets hot. They work great and you'll immediately double your countertop space, because you can use it when the stove isn't on.

Airlines have the screwiest pricing schedules of anything you'll ever encounter. For the same flight, a business passenger sitting next to you may have paid up to $400 less for his ticket than you did -- for the exact same transportation! To beat this, when using an online service such as Travelocity.com or Expedia.com, don't put in your exact flying dates at first. Rather, put in that your dates are flexible -- you'll often find that the exact dates you need are available much cheaper than if you had specified precise departure/return days. Don't ask me why, but it's true.

A lot of people sleep better with white noise in the room. To me, it's impossible to drift away in a deathly silent bedroom, since I'm always hearing every creak and crack of the house. So I use a space heater on the "fan only" setting. The soft static noise blankets the minor racket going on in the house, and I can get some rest. You can spend hundreds on babbling brook sounds and crashing waves and chirping birds, but the simple and plain background hum of the space heater (fan only) works great for me.

Buying media. They want $30 for some new hardback books nowadays! Forget that! Instead, find the book you want on Amazon.com and then click on "available used". You can find the most amazing and incredible bargains. Books that were bestsellers a year or two ago are now 50 cents and a dollar through Amazon.com's Used Dept.! These are small booksellers who typically charge you three or four dollars for shipping, but the book itself is often peanuts! And the quality is very very high, I've never been disappointed with a book I've purchased from Amazon used, they are often brand spanking new. Of course, you might also find what you want at the library, for free.

Use Oil Lamps instead of candles. Oil Lamps come in a million decorative sizes, shapes and colors and they burn all night on an ounce of Lamp Oil. Oil Lamps won't flame out in the wind, they can be hung from most anywhere and they are much brighter than candles since they use a fat wick instead of a tiny wick. The Lamp Oil itself is actually paraffin (wax!) and will not burn on it's own, so it's very safe. Buy the most expensive Lamp Oil you can (about $3/quart) to eliminate even the smallest of odors.

You want a boat? Rent one or join one of those clubs that charge you a couple of hundred dollars a month to borrow one of their boats whenever you want. A boat will cost you more in maintenance the first two years than you spent buying it. They say that the 2nd happiest day in a boater's life is when he buys the boat. The first happiest day is when he sells it.

Get TiVO. I don't care which model you get, what your cable company offers in digital video recorders, or what people who don't have one tell you: Get TiVO. Your life will improve immensely. You'll actually spend *less* time watching television because you only watch exactly what you want to, exactly *when* you want to, without commercials. Get TiVO. Another thing, turn on Closed Captioning. With many movies you can watch the movie in double-time while reading the closed captions. The fast forward options on TiVO are 2X, 8X and 60X. 60X means that a minute of programming goes by for ever second of fast forwarding. Three minutes of commercials are *gone* in 3 seconds. The slow motion/freeze-frame features and programming guides are *awesome.* Want to record every Seinfeld that comes on, no matter what channel or what time of day? Just get a "Season Pass" and the next thing you know there will be 40 Seinfeld episodes waiting for you. The Guide is Awesome. Too many features to enumerate here, but trust me: Get TiVO.

More on TiVO: One more astonishing thing you'll learn is how much material is on basic cable. It's vast. Hundreds of movies, thousands of shows, all easily located using TiVo's Guide. Punch in your favorite actor, and ever movie or show that person appears on will be brought to your attention for viewing. It's truly jaw-dropping.

Get your kids computers *early*! While in Kindergarten, if not pre-school. An entry level Macintosh will do perfectly. It doesn't matter what they use it for (they'll use it for games) but they'll benefit *immensely* throughout their lives with the computer skills they'll learn. By grade school they'll be a wiz. By middle school they'll be as good as any adult employee working a job today. A computer in their lives is far more educational than TV or video games, and at first they'll only play what you buy them (and you'll buy them Jump Start school games, won't you?) I don't recommend giving them internet access until middle school, and *then* you need to put blockers on it, or at least turn Google Preferences to *strict* to keep the crap out. And don't let them have email until high school. You know what's best. Enforce it.

Don't use a stock broker, no matter how much they court you and make you feel like a big shot. If they knew anything about the stock market they wouldn't need your money.

You didn't hear it from me, but I think the IRS just opens the envelopes and takes out the checks and cashes them.

Don't overpay the IRS through payroll deductions, that's like hiding cash under a rock for a year when you could be earning interest.

There are only two "Herbal" products I know of that work, one is 5-HTP, which adds serotonin to your brain. It puts you in good spirits and reduces depression-like attitudes. If you feel happier, you'll work happier and be more successful. Subtle, but effective over time. Melatolin also does great at making you feel sleepy and relaxed. Consult your doctor first so I don't get sued if something happens!

This is something I heard once I've never forgotten: "Some people run away to find happiness, only to find that it was happiness they ran away from."

You can't hit the jackpot if you don't gamble.

If you quit before you win, you will lose every time.

Learn basic body language techniques. Looking down means they're lying, looking up means they're searching for an answer, arms crossed means "stay away" or "I'm hiding something", covering their mouth while they speak means know they should be saying what they're saying. Get a book about it.

Google can quickly correct your spelling! Type in a difficult-to-spell word the best way you can, and Google will come back with (for example) "Did you mean '*gymnastics*'?"

Get a moped! For trips around the neighborhood to the grocery or drug store, there's nothing more fun. Most are large enough for two people, especially an adult and a grandchild! Your kids will love riding around (make sure they wear a helmet) I'm on my second Tomos Sprint (I burned out the first one at 23,000 miles). I don't have to mention how much gasoline and wear and tear you'll save on your car, just using the moped for short trips. Mine gets 80 miles per gallon -- beat that!

Eat out a lunch instead of dinner. Most restaurants have an equally delicious lunch menu as they do dinner, and the prices will be at least half. Lunching out is also a good way to try out a new restaurant without spending a fortune.

Before making a purchase, do the math and figure out how many hours you had to work to earn the money to buy that item. Is it worth it?

How to avoid impulse buying: Sometimes I'll pick up an item I want to buy but know it's too expense and frivolous, so I just carry it around the store, as if I'm going to buy it. By the time I'm ready to check out, I've gotten over the idea that I was going to buy that item and I put it back, saving the wasteful expense! The impulse fades after "pretending" you're going to buy it.

Be careful who you listen to. For example, nationally syndicated talk show host, Dr. Phil, is a fat man aggressively selling his weight loss and diet book... so *What's that tell you*?

Never take the extra insurance for a rental car, because you're already fully covered by your own car insurance. It's just a free bit of cash for the car rental agency. Keep it in your pocket instead. And *always* return the rental car full of gas -- otherwise they charge you double the going rate per gallon for the convenience of filling it up for you.

If you like traveling dangerously (such as without a reservation for a hotel), then when it's time to check in some place, choose a hotel that doesn't look busy. When they quote you a room price for the night, cut the figure in half and say these magic words "I'll take one of your vacancies at X price (half what was quoted), or can you direct me to a nearby hotel with lower rates?" Most of the time, you'll get the half price rate -- because hotels are businesses, and when rooms sit empty overnight, they don't make a dime. In fact, they lose money because housekeeping won't be cleaning the empty rooms, yet they get paid anyway. Also, it's smart to telephone the hotel from a cell or pay phone (even if your in sight of it!), ask for the standard room rate, then ask for an upgrade at the same price. They don't know you're close to checking in, so they very often will agree to the free upgrade just to get you in.

If you've never taken a cruise, do it! Choose the largest and newest ship you can. Exploring the ship and it's numerous luxury features and services is 33% the fun. Save money by booking early -- you'll often get automatically upgraded on the room as the sailing date approaches. Alternately, you can call around the cruise lines at the last minute and ask for good deals for spur-of-the-moment travelers. If you insist on having a window (port hole!) you'll pay extra for it, but believe me, inside cabins with no windows are just as nice, and you'll only be using your room for sleeping and changing clothes. Cruise ships start early -- there's nothing like walking the deck with a fresh cup of coffee at dawn. For later in the evening, you might be using the cheap no-tax duty-free booze you bought onshore. Even if you're not a cigar person, you might enjoy firing up a Cuban once just to see what the thrill is all about. Cuban cigars are perfectly legal and abundant outside the United States.

Reserve your room in the center of a block of rooms, rather than near major hallways or entrances to the quarters -- it will be much quieter at night when all the teens are roaming around hooping and hollering.

Casinos on cruise ships are generally far more lax and friendly than on shore. The dealers are typically funny and out-going while they take your money, instead of stoic and robotic as you'll generally find elsewhere. But beware -- only Vegas has the Nevada

Gaming Commission to keep things scrupulously honest. You won't find loose slots or Player's Clubs or freebies.

When you take your 2nd cruise, don't make the mistake we did to go on the same ship again -- the memories come back quickly, and like I said, exploring the ship is 33% the fun.

Another cruise tip: Don't buy souvenirs in the gift shop window until the last day of the cruise -- when everything goes on sale!

If you are given the opportunity to take an all expense paid vacation with the catch being you have to sit through a "presentation" for a "time share" or other fee-based membership, it's never really worth it. They'll be on you like locust, the promised free stuff is generally so-so or even sub-standard. They'll stick you in a room with high pressure sales people -- it's really not worth the time or trouble, in my view.

Don't "stock up" on your inkjet printer's ink. It will dry up and be useless before you get to the last of it.

DVD Rent-By-Mail services. Just realize that every-body wants to see the same new movies, so you'll be waiting weeks for your turn in line. And the farther away from the distribution point, the longer your DVDs will take to arrive and go back -- reducing the number of DVDs you can rent per month, even though it's "unlimited".

Briefly about buying a house: Always have your own, personally-hired Real Estate Attorney go over the papers before you sign. Sometimes they make no changes, but if the mortgager knows that the paper-work will be examined prior to your signing, that alone is enough for them to keep off the trickery. Also, hire your own Appraiser to evaluate your potential house. Don't let the seller recommend his brother-in-law.

When in College or going back to school for an advanced degree, always buy used textbooks. They're often 50% cheaper and they're usually already highlighted and marked up for you!

If you're all fired-up to get some home exercise equipment to get into tip-top shape, first check the classifieds or eBay Local to find the gizmo you're interested in. Over 70% of people who buy tread-mills or weights or other contraptions don't use them for more than a few weeks -- then they sell them off. You'll find some good bargains in used equipment.

Don't be scared or fooled by in-house "collection agencies". Any vendor who sends you a frightening or sternly worded letter is actually telling you that he has no other option but to try to intimidate you into paying. Elapsed magazine subscriptions, cancelled pay-per-month purchases from TV infomercials have no recourse legally. They can't sue. They can't hurt your credit (they don't even know your social security number, do they?). The law in most states educates us that any item sent to us in the mail should be either paid for prior to shipping, or 100% free. Some scams involve sending you a useless trinket and then having computer-generated bills and invoices hound you every two weeks. Just throw them away. Firms can't legally mail you a brick you didn't ask for and then try to charge you fifty bucks for it. Just remember it's only a computer hassling you. They'll stop when they've figured out you're never going to pay.

Do not ever *ever* get a "Paycheck Loan" or "Payday Advance". They'll bury you quickly. If you borrow $200 this week from next week's paycheck, they'll charge you $240 and you're just as bad off as you were the week before -- and $40 poorer because of the interest. It's a vicious trap outlawed in many states. And for good reason.

Don't rent furniture or TVs or Stereos. Do the math! By the time you rent-to-own the mediocre merchandise, you'll have paid four times it's retail price. Even if your only going to be in town for a few months and you need to furnish an apartment, either lease a furnished apartment in the first place, or buy some used stuff from the classifieds. You'll pay 90% less and still have a place to sit and a table to eat at.

If you need to break a lease for an apartment, don't just leave. First find out what the penalty is (it's sometimes very reasonable). But if you do skip and they try to come after you, the law varies state by state on what they can actually do to you. Find out what the transient laws are that cover this type of thing. Generally, if you vacate an apartment all you'll lose is your security deposit (which you probably weren't expecting to get back anyway).

If you want to visit a psychic as a gag, that's fine -- but beware that all they are doing is asking you questions and hoping to hit some facts in your life they can expound on. No psychic is real. No psychic has any special powers or insight. If they did, they would be working for the government or warning of disasters, they wouldn't be trying to get your twenty bucks. The most unscrupulous psychic frauds will trick weak-minded people into believing a curse is on their head, and say that for only $10,000 (or more) the psychic will perform a ritual to remove it. (You didn't think psychics made a living *only* on $20 readings, did you?)

When you buy new tires, what they don't tell you is that if you rotate them (put the front tires on the rear, move the rear tires to the front) will double the life of your tread. The front tires wear much faster because of all the high speed turning. It's commonly agreed that you have your tires rotated every 6,000 miles, or every other oil change.

If you can't pay cash for your new car (the best way), then go to your bank and get pre-approved for an automobile loan with fixed payments (not adjustable payments). Your bank won't cheat you, they'll charge you the fair and going interest rate and put you into the appropriate term of months. Car dealerships, on the other hand, will try all manor of sleazy trickery, such as telling you your credit is poor so you have to pay higher rates, adding in additional bogus fees and dubious services to add to the cost of the loan. They'll even try to call you back into the dealership three days after you bought the car with a phone call "Good news! We were able to get your payments lowered - come on in and sign the new paperwork!" What they really did was increase the term of the loan by adding a year or two to it, which has the effect of lowering your monthly payment, but in the long run you pay 20% to 40% more. Car salesman are demons, and sales managers are Satan himself. The best and funniest and most informative book I've read on the subject is called "How to Buy A New Car And Not Get Taken Every Time." It's written like a novel, with "Killer" being the main character, a crack salesman who demonstrates in the story evil trick after evil trick as average people -- who only want a new car -- get conned over and over again. (Tip: get this book used on Amazon.com for about $2.00. The author is Remar Sutton)

We most regret the things we didn't do, never the things we did.

On children: I've heard this more than once, "If I had to do it all over again I've have a dozen of them. It's all you really have when you get old."

When meeting new people, you'll judged by how they size up your appearance. In other words, they judge the book by its cover -- until proven otherwise. Sometimes you can use this to your advantage. For example, go shopping for new cars wearing ratty clothing. If you show up looking like a million bucks they'll try to take that much from you.

Poor people (or people who appear poor) get better deals.

Kurt Vonnegut said that happiness comes from the fulfillment of childhood dreams. So, if you always wanted to eat an entire can of chocolate frosting, do it!

George Bernard Shaw said "Youth is wasted on the young." Well, you're as young today as you're ever going to be -- do something grand with it.

While driving through a "bad" area of town, I noticed that the Air Pump at the gas stations cost 25 cents. Up in my area, which happens to be much much nicer, the Air Pump at the gas stations cost 75 cents. And so I realized that even in the coin-operated air pump business, you can only charge what the market will bear.

Always have something going on the side. I think this is crucial to financial success these days. When I young, I had a paper route *and* I mowed lawns. Later, in college, I tutored students in lower classes. When I had a full-time job, I bought used TVs cheap and re-sold them at the flea market on weekends at a higher price. Here's where I can plug Linky & Dinky's Web Earner Guide: make money on the internet using only your point/click skills and a bit of common sense.
http://www.linkydinky.com/JobDescription.shtml
The point being is that when one stream of income dries up, you won't.

You can solve almost any problem through trial and error. That's the crux of what evolution is, and it worked pretty well, didn't it?

You are no more likely to hit it big in the stock market than you are to win the lottery or draw a royal flush in video poker. I'll say it again: if stock brokers knew what they were doing (as they insist) they wouldn't need your money. Stock brokers don't make money when stocks rise or fall, instead, they make money when YOU buy or sell a stock through the brokerage. It's called "churning". The more they can convince you a stock has topped and should be sold, or that another stock has bottomed and should be bought -- they make money on your transaction. You're taking all the risk.

I like these lyrics to a Johnny Mathis song:
Dreams make promises they can't keep,
They can swindle us while we sleep,
and the morning finds us wondering why.
It seems when we're young in dreams we trust,
maybe growing up is just
kissing certain dreams goodbye.

You'll never forget the first time a kid calls you "Sir" or "Ma'am". It's a turning point, psychologically.

I try not to buy anything from anybody who is trying to sell it to me. Be it gold coins, heating oil, timeshares, pizza coupons, mutual funds, club memberships, exercise equipment, etc. because I just think that anything worth buying doesn't have to be "sold".

There are lots of tricks used by people to sell us stuff. Tupperware makes a trillion dollars a year getting housewives to host parties -- because who can turn down buying from your friend who invited you into her home? Charities send us calendars and peel/stick labels and other nonsense in the mail so we'll feel guilty about accepting the gift -- so we pay them back with something... usually a donation.

We get our deepest sleep the first hour of resting. So, if you typically sleep 6 or 7 hours straight through, you'll actually get MORE rest if you wake up, get up, do something for 20 minutes, then go back to bed -- you'll get a 2nd deep first hour of sleep.

If your own snoring starts to keep you awake, meaning that as soon as you nod off your snoring pops you back awake again in a repeating cycle, this can be very frustrating. It's because you gained weight. Lose a pound or two and this won't happen anymore.

High blood pressure DOES have symptoms! You feel keyed up, an internal pressure, your mind is uneasy. See your doctor if you know you have high blood pressure for medications. The medication nowadays has little or no side effects, and you WILL feel much better (as well as live longer).

This one tidbit alone may change your life: Flushable baby wipes. Works great on kids *and* grown-ups.

If you're not saving at least 20% of your income you're never going to make it. You can't start yesterday or last year or 10 years ago, so start today. Put 20% in an account and leave it there, be poorer, skip restaurants, whatever, but you must save 20% or eventually you'll be living with your adult children. Social Security won't even pay for your medicine, don't rely on it.

I find that clear, empty floor space is more important and valuable than the junk that was there before. Just throw things out, give them to friends or Goodwill. You can easily go through your house and eliminate 20% of what's stuffed in corners and filling drawers and closets. The remaining empty space will please you.

Pickpockets are every bit as good as you've seen in the movies. They look like nobody, you'll never remember their faces, in most cases you won't even know they swiped your stuff until hours later. When in crowds, especially public travel areas, theme parks (yes! They know you're loaded with cash while on vacation), airports, concerts, even office lobbies and city streets, keep your wallet in your front pocket. *I* can't hardly get my wallet out of my front pocket, so neither can they. Purses should be under your arm or slung around the other shoulder.

"Just spell the name right" goes the old saying. And in this internet age, it's a little different: "Just spell the URL right." For goodness sakes, if somebody links to your web site, but you don't care for the comment they made about it, don't berate them or flame them! Just be glad they got your URL out

there. It really doesn't matter, in fact, the more controversial the better -- as long as they spelled your URL correctly, then leave it be. By the way, a URL is the web site address, like mine, http://www.linkydinky.com   It's all about traffic, your web site will stand on it's own.

Don't buy cheap paint. It's thinner, you'll have to buy twice as much of it to cover the same space with multiple coats.

Consumer Reports warns: Plasma TVs have a usable lifespan of only 3 years, versus 10 years for LCD screens and 50 years for the old-fashioned CRT.

Get yourself subscribed to some sort of credit monitoring services. Equifax has one that I use, you'll get an email the same day *any* new information is added to your credit report. Invaluable in stopping identity theft in the bud.

Believe it or not (look it up) you can't stuff yourself to the feeling of "full" very quickly. It takes about 20 minutes for your brain to register enough food in your stomach to reduce hunger pangs, so eat slowly and you won't eat as much. *Anything* on this topic is a help.

A joke you made up will come across much funnier to your audience if you first attribute it to someone known to be funny, for example: "Jerry Seinfeld said..."

Jumping between projects, leaving each unfinished, will likely leave both never completed. Work on one project at a time until it's done. This can also go for Cellphone use in the car, for which a true life-saving bumpersticker was invented: "SHUT UP AND DRIVE".

You should read the directions and menu suggestions on the boxes of prepared food you buy. Sometimes you'll really like the ideas the have.

When someone offers you a deal, immediately and *instantly* counter-offer for your side. For example, someone might say "I'll buy your lunch if you go pickup the food." You quickly come back with, "OK, but that's going to include a dessert too!" They'll most often easily agree. Whatever they offer you, bump it up. Do it as a habit, little by little your benefits will add up.

I read somewhere that the odds of getting a traffic ticket for running a red light are 50 to 1, but the odds of getting killed while running a red light are only 20 to 1.

When separating a dessert for kids, like chocolate cake: have one kid cut the pieces in half, let the other kid choose which one he wants. You'll never see a more fair cut!

Store your family photographs and movies and letters and kid's school work in a fireproof box -- those things are the among the most important items in your house, no amount of "contents" insurance can replace them.

You've heard that laughter is contagious, just like yawning. But so are arguing, bitter comments and insults. Don't be the one to start a round of those!

Dehydration can cause many pains that are misinterpreted as something else, like hunger, arthritis, headache, stiffness, etc. Drink a bunch of water. Keep a gallon of pure distilled water in the refrigerator, or get one of those water bottle cooler dispensers for your home, it will remind and encourage you to drink more. I couldn't live without mine.

Two tennis balls tossed into the dryer with your wet clothes will make them dry 10% to 15% faster, due to the randomized movement and separation of the clothing.

Back in my day it was always said that a fool and his money is soon parted. Nowadays, it happens to everyone.

Time is all you have. It amazes me that people who want to live forever can't occupy themselves on a rainy Sunday afternoon.

To determine a man's true talent for organization, watch him mow a lawn.

Don't be so afraid of the bad things that you miss the good things.

Another attitude perk-me-up idea -- don't be frustrated that roses have thorns, be happy the thorns have roses.

Practical joke: If someone in your house "believes" in ghosts, plan this vicious little trick. Start very slowly placing a penny here and there around the house in spots that person frequents. Put a penny in her shoe one day, the next day put a penny near the sink. Wait a day, put one on the floor of her car where she'll see it. Put a penny in one of her pockets. On the 5th or 6th day, start placing two pennies in a pile in even more unusual places. At this point, she will probably mention to you that she's been finding pennies in odd places. Act disinterested. The next day, put a pile of 4 or 5 pennies on a bookshelf or her night-stand. This will cause her to freak and come running to tell you. Raise your eyes to the sky and start to "remember" that you heard one time that deceased loved ones often leave pennies around to tell you that they love you and are watching out for you. You'll have to be the best judge of when to do the finale: put a handful of pennies in her bed under-neath the covers. At this point, she'll scream and you can come clean. Warning: don't do this unless you're willing to be taken to task *or* if she can't handle the joke.

Here's some advice: don't give advice. You should probably make an exception if the person will be hurting themselves badly if you don't share your wisdom, but otherwise, let them learn from their own mistakes. That's the best teacher.

I'm continually perplexed by the world's failure to end as prophesied.

I have tested and retested the Golden Rule, but in the end, there's no money in it. Sure, it brings peace and happiness, but no hard cash. Maybe the Silver Rule will be more profitable.

Did Adam and Eve have belly buttons? Think about it.

I remember when Linky & Dinky were young, and how they started out hanging around grocery stores for hours, passing out cool links on toothpicks. Look at them now! Nearly half a million weekly readers, all captivated not by what Linky & Dinky do, but by what they find. Granted, the writing has a lot to do with it, but even so, it just goes to show you that great things can happen if you just stick to it. Of course, if Linky & Dinky hadn't been successful, you'd never be reading this book!

People go where people are.

After you have used Crest's flavorful smooth viscous compound in conjunction with a bristled implement to abrasively remove the build-up of foul, mucky matter and grime from the hard bonelike structures rooted in sockets in your jaws, don't immediately eat Oreos.

Don't teach your kids to distinguish one type of snake from another so they'll know which one is poisonous, teach them to run from all snakes!

Chaos theory, a hoiti toiti mathematical idea, states that a butterfly's flapping wings can eventually cause a hurricane on the opposite side of the planet. So, I hear that, and I have to ask them "Butterflys, yes, you may be right, but what about dog farts? What would they cause 'eventually'?"

Butterflies were originally called Flutterbys. Why in the world would they change that beautiful name?

"Lies, damned lies, and statistics" goes the saying. If you need to dazzle someone, use statistics. I believe I heard one time that 130% (nearly half!) of all people don't understand statistics.

The first science team to invent a placebo which cures hypochondria will win millions!

My inner child is at that fun age, where I'm going to do whatever I want. That's the only good thing about growing old.

I think if aliens ever land on the White House lawn the first thing they're going to say is "listen up people, you all need to go on low fat, high fiber diets and start exercising."

Would somebody please invent a salt aerosol to spray in the kitchen so dinner would smell better?

No matter what anybody tells you, most often in life saying "what the hell!" turns out to be the right decision.

Please allow me to point out, just because I find it curious, that with all the evidence of UFOs in the form of photos, video, radar scans, eyewitness sightings, artifacts on the ground -- even the cameras on the Space Shuttle that have recorded UFO events -- people still poo-poo the existence of extraterrestrial beings because the evidence just isn't good enough. Well, that's far more substantiation than the evidence supporting the existence of God or Allah or any afterlife world, yet people buy into those ancient campfire stories like crazy. I'm afraid that Earth is never going to be invited to join the Federation of Planets if we don't wise up!

As new parents, you'll worry and fret over the thousands of seemingly odd and unusual things your newborn child will do (or not do, or smell like, or not smell like.) Every question you ask will be answered by the professionals with a "that's normal". Your baby is fine. Just keep in mind ancient cave babies. They grew up and thrived without Dr. Spock or modern medicine -- your baby has all those advantages, so don't worry, just enjoy them.

Would somebody please invent a trick chess set, so I can win once in a while?

Crop circles: If crop circles were from aliens, they wouldn't bother with complex indecipherable geometric patterns, they'd just write "*eat less you fat earthlings*".

Why does God ignore sports-related prayers?

Any idea which works, no matter how crazy it is, is a good idea. Conversely, a boomerang that doesn't work is called a stick.

Don't fret about all the things you think you'll have to buy when you have your first baby -- the fact is, family and friends and neighbors will flood you items, you'll virtually spend nothing on clothing or toys or decorations. Be sure to register with Formula and Diaper companies, they will send you reams of coupons for their products.

Headaches: if you feel a headache coming on, take whatever pain relief you usually do *right away*. Your Tylenol (or other) will be more effective when it has a head start -- less pain to kill, you see. A headache in the late afternoon might be nixed with a simple cup of coffee. Give it a try. Backfire warning: if your body gets used to two or three cups of coffee a day, don't just stop. You'll get terrible headaches and other pains from the withdrawal.

Don't swig from your old water bottle you had left on your bike or in your car or at your desk. Since the last time you drank from it, which could have been 24 hours ago, bacteria from your mouth has grown into awful mutated bugs. You'll get sick. Don't drink from a water bottle in warm weather over 2 or 3 hours old.

Almost every over-the-counter remedy or drug has sitting on the shelf right next to it a generic equivalent with a weird name. Here's an easy test: find the $12 bottle of Tylenol on your grocer's shelf, then look right next to it you'll find a generic acetaminophen with exactly, precisely the same ingredients for $4.00. It's like that with most remedies for sale.

When leaving a public restroom, grab a paper towel and use it to keep your clean hands off that filthy door handle. Look behind the door (near the hinge) you'll see where other people have done this and discarded the paper towel on their way out.

Try eating your favorite meal while wearing a blind-fold. Without being able to see the yummy food, you'll eat up to a third less naturally. It's the visual cues of a full plate that make us stuff ourselves. You can also try physically smaller dinner plates to mask the smaller portions.

Long walks or bike rides will go a lot faster if your brain is occupied. Rather than music, which might make you want to relax, instead listen to a good Book on Tape -- or -- my favorite, Coast to Coast AM. This is an overnight radio show in all 50 states that Art Bell began and still hosts on weekends. Topics are wide ranging and always fascinating. Get a radio record from CCrane.com (the VersaCorder records 4 hours of audio on one side of a cassette tape) or just download the MP3 files from www.coastto-coastam.com. You can download the MP3 files directly to your iPod or equivalent. I use the RadioYourWay from CCrane, it's a radio-recordermp3 player all in one and with fantastic sound on earphones. Anyway, that's what I do, so I recommend it.

Stop trying to find the closest parking spot. Park far away and walk (weather allowing). It's better for your heart, lungs, muscles, circulation, and general health. Plus, you'll always find a parking spot at the edge of the mall.

The George Foreman grill makes awful hamburgers for the simple fact that it does what it says it does: drain away the fat. However, it is *fantastic for* cooking a frozen steak. The cooking time is quick, 7 to 11 minutes, and it will be nice and red and juicy inside (if you like it rare to medium rare). Always start frozen, so that the outside will be nice and toasted prior to the center cooking. If you start with a de-thawed steak the outside color will be pale brown and awful looking (but will still taste good.)

Why do Casino's have table limits? Because it makes you play longer, and the longer you play, the Law of Averages works in their favor, so the longer you play, the more likely you are to lose.

There's a trick to winning Blackjack (besides just knowing the card hit/stand rules). It's called "progressive", meaning that when you lose a hand, double the size of the next bet. If you win that hand, you're back to where you started without having lost anything. But if you lose again, you need to double again (quadrupling your original bet). If you win, you're back to where you started, if you lose... double the chips again. However, eventually you'll reach the table limit and your night at the gaming tables is over because you're broke!

If you're late on a credit card bill once in a blue moon, just call the credit card company and usually they'll wipe off the late fee.

Debt Consolidation will take all your bills and swirl them into a new loan for a much longer term. This has the effect of lowering your monthly payments (yippy!) but in the long run you'll end up paying 20% to 30% more in hard cash.

Things not to tell children about money: 1. "We Can't Afford It" *They know that's not true.* 2. "Money Is The Root Of All Evil" Actually, it's the *love* of money that is the root of all evil. 3. "Time Is Money Don't Waste It" teaches them that everything is based on money.

There is no "standard" rate for life insurance. If you get 10 quotes, you'll get 10 vastly different fees. I always pick the middle one for a nice balance of benefits vs. cost. Buy "term" insurance rather than "whole life". Whole Life is sold as a savings account that you can cash out later -- put your money in the bank instead, you'll earn more interest.

Make sure you get replacement cost on your home owner's insurance, even though they'll try to talk you out of it. After a few years your home might be worth 50% to 100% more in value, yet if it burns down, you only get the original value of your house. It'll ruin you.

If you have a car accident and don't report it to the police, no matter how minor it is, your insurance company can nix the benefit. If the cost of collision insurance is more than 6% the value of your car then cancel it. It will save you 25% on insurance premiums! You can find the value of your car at www.kbb.com

Paying off your home mortgage should be the LAST thing you pay off. Get completely rid of credit cards, car loans, school loans -- everything -- before you even think about reducing your home mortgage. It's a good idea to pay additional each month to save you $1,000s in interest, but not when you're paying a much higher rate on other loans.

I'm no tax expert, but here's some things you probably didn't know you could deduct: prescription drugs, weight-loss programs, stop-smoking programs, alternative treatments (including massages!), health insurance premiums if you are self-employed, nursing home expenses, travel associated with health care, home improvements and paid day care or pre-school expenses, school expenses, a hybrid car, exercise equipment if you are classified obese, adoption and a bunch of others.

If anybody tries to give you something for free, but they require *any* money up front first, it's a scam. They might call it "money transfer fees", "bank fees", "taxes", "transportation", whatever -- Free is free, and if it's not, they're trying to scam you.

Electronic filing scam: If you pay someone to file your return and you opt to collect your tax refund electronically, the tax preparer can put their own bank account information on the form so *they* collect your refund. If you miss this trick and sign the form anyway, you cannot get reparations... you signed your tax return under oath, so legally it's what you intended to do, there's nothing you can do about it.

Have you heard ads on the radio about donating your old car or boat or RV to a charity? Don't do it -- that's a red flag for a tax audit since you probably (most likely!) entered a figure higher than the IRS thinks is accurate. If you want to make a donation, just donate it. Don't mix in the IRS.

No advertisement on TV for an automobile dealership has ever been truthful or accurate. You'll never *ever* get the deal that sounds so wonderful.

Getting bargains: A Harris Poll conducted in 2002 found that 14% of consumers routinely, habitually, ask the store manager for a discount before making a significant purchase, the result being that half the time their request for a markdown was granted. Tip: don't ask for the discount within earshot of other customers, they don't want to start an impromptu sale. The rule of thumb is always ask (politely) for a break on the price. Some examples of what to say... "Can you do better on this price?" "That price is too high, what's the lowest you'll go?" "How much will you reduce this if I buy it right now?" If they refuse, just walk out. He might catch you on the way out with a counter-offer before the door slams close behind you.

Bill paying trick with mortgages and credit cards: pay half your monthly payment every two weeks instead of in full once a month. You'll save a ton in interest and actually make two extra payments per year without noticing it -- the final payoff will come 75% faster than if you stick with monthly payments!

Do a blind taste test with any bottle water brand you choose against the tap water -- most of the time you'll never taste any difference, or might even prefer the tap water. Why? Tap water comes from a municipality that employs many people to constantly check on water quality. Bottled water doesn't have any legal obligation to be better or purer than tap water and is usually just filtered tap water anyway. They sell it because it's in a nice bottle with a fancy label. Imagine charging your friends a dollar for a glass of water when they come to visit!

When trying to find something on eBay, always check the misspellings. Often an item is listed with a common spelling error, meaning that fewer people will see it -- meaning less competition for you on bidding! Also, when selling on eBay, time your auction to close on Sunday night when by far the most people are online browsing eBay.

If you want to return an item you purchased, but can't find the receipt -- bring your credit card or debit card receipt to the store. They'll usually accept it.

Cheap, independent carpet cleaners are often scammers, quoting you one price on the phone and then upping charges all over the place for moving furniture, using detergent or scotchgard, etc. And often their equipment is rented or of weak, poor quality. Hire a national brand and insist on a pre-cleaning inspecting for an accurate quote, and make them explain the charges. Never rent those handheld units at the grocery store, they are only as hot as the hot water you add to them and their suction power is several orders of magnitude *less* than the truck-mounted units.

Be obsessed about changing the air conditioner filter in your house. Once you see any lint or dust build up, replace it. Every particle of dust on that filter takes money right out of your wallet. Filters are cheap, energy isn't.

If you use free internet services such as www.repair-clinic.com you can get a real good idea what's wrong with your appliance before you call a potentially dishonest repairman. You might even learn enough to be able to fix the problem yourself, paying only for parts (you can get most parts for anything at Sears or other appliance repair stores.

If you really want to get depressed, use the quick calculator at www.asec.org/ballpark to show you how much money you need to start saving per year *now* to be able to afford a reasonably comfortable retirement. Not thinking about retiring? Too bad, because the younger you start the better off you'll be, gramps.

Make a photocopy of the front and back of all your credit cards, driver's license and any other important ID you have. If you lose them, or they are stolen, you'll have the information you need to get them replaced (and cancelled, in the case of credit cards!).

Meeting people trick. Tons of years ago, I was at a crowded bar with a couple of friends when these two girls came up to our table and and said "Hi, I'm Rachel, this is Sherri, it's nice to meet you, we're trying to meet everybody!" Super icebreaker. I married one of them!

A paranoid worry you might have, that everybody poo-poos, which turns out to be correct, is then hailed as "good thinking"!

The World Bank is a protection racket. You hear about the World Bank, but never knew what it does. It's like the mob: they go into third world countries who are mostly barefoot, living in Tiki Huts, and then loan them an enormous amount of money they couldn't possibly hope to repay. The trick is: that poor country has something valuable, like oil or diamonds or gold! The World Bank hires global companies to go in and build roads and electrical power plants and other infrastructure (all paid for out of the original loan). Years later, when the poor country still can't pay, the World Bank makes them mine or drill their untapped resources and then buys that commodity from them at substantially reduced prices. In that way, the poor country has some income to pay off the loan! After a few decades, the poor country wises up and balks at the tactic, so the World Bank "forgives" the loan, but by that time they've been repaid many many times over. That's why you never see truly poor countries like Haiti or Rhwanda get loans, they don't have collateral!

Travel with cheap, beat up luggage. It's less of a target to thieves.

Keep your children's most interesting or unique toys, especially those based on new cartoon characters. Years from now, today's forgotten toy in the attic may be worth big bucks.

Most TV dinners are already 100% fully cooked, so in the event of extended loss of electrical power, you can eat them newly thawed. Of course, you'll have to be really really hungry to go this route!

When stopped in a traffic jam, put your car in neutral instead of leaving it in Drive with the brake pressed. This will reduce pressure on your transmission. Also, if you know you'll be idling for more than two minutes, turn the engine off. While idling you're getting zero miles per gallon and potentially over-heating the car.

Don't mix ammonia and bleach, or use them one after the other on a cleaning project. Ammonia and bleach together generate mustard gas! The very same used in World War I!

What do the Life Insurance companies know that we don't know? With their actuary tables and statistics and black magic, they've figured out a bunch of death-foretelling signs and use them to determine Life Insurance rates. A friend of mine who was in that business for decades spilled the beans:

a. Take a deep deep breath and hold it. If your chest is still smaller in diameter than your belly, you're 60% more likely to die young from over-weight health problems.

b. Smoke? 200% more likely to die before age 75.

c. Did both parents die from health reason before age 60? There's a 30% chance you will too.

d. Fat people don't commit suicide anywhere near the rate that skinny people do.

e. Nearsighted people have more psychological issues, including anxiety, phobia and depression, than the farsighted.

f. This one is obvious: the wealthy live longer because they get better health care, and more often.

g. The best occupation to live a long life? Farmer, college professor and minister.

h. There is a 10% chance you'll catch a new infection while in the hospital being treated for something else, and 20% of those are fatal. The advice here: stay out of the hospital!

Write down the actual drug name and dosage that your doctor prescribed, and check it against the pill bottle you get from the pharmacist. Estimates are that 3-5% of filled prescriptions are wrong due to misreading the doctor's handwriting on the script.

Get rid of any aluminum cooking pots, pans or utensils. The slow buildup of aluminum in your system is cumulative and has been shown to lead to memory loss, dementia and alzheimer's disease.

Try to schedule big item purchases such as a new car, house, refrigerator, recreational vehicle, sprinkler system, roofing, etc. during the period between Christmas and Valentine's Day. Buyers are scarce during that time due to vacations, snow, credit card blues from Christmas shopping and so forth. You'll get the best deals and not have to wait long for service!

The absolute best way to make your used car look like a million bucs is to have the engine steam/pressure cleaned. You can do it yourself with a high pressure hose, simply heavily spray the engine area down first with a good Tire Wheel cleaner, the kind used to remove brake dust from the rims. The water won't hurt it, but if your spark plug wires are cracked you'll get some arcing or stalling until the water is evaporated. But after you're done the engine will shine and be colorful and truly convince anyone (even you!) there's a 100,000 miles worth of life left in it!

If your car is overheating after a long highway drive or steep mountain climbing, turn the heater on full blast. This directly removes heat from the engine and helps tremendously -- you'll be able to see the temperature gauge fall. Of course, you might need to open the windows during this time...

Does your bicycle seat really hurt?
I solved this problem with a bizarre seat from:
http://www.spiderflex.com
No more pain at all, no more discomfort at all, no more pinched nerves or numbness at all. No amount of padding or fat/wide seating gizmos will reduce

the pain. With my Spiderflex seat I can ride for hours and hours (and do!) in perfect comfort. And that's the fact, jack.

Guaranteed sleeping trick: Tense, and then relax, individual parts of your body (hands, legs, thighs, neck, shoulders, etc.) and concentrate and force that area to completely relax. By the time you've made the rounds you should be well on your way to sleeping. Alternately, start a dream! If you like flying dreams, begin an imaginary trip through the forest flying amongst the trees. The longer you can continue the dream, the closer you are to actual sleep.

Bananas can be kept in the refrigerator for a week or even more -- the peel will turn brown, but the meat will remain as crispy and tender as when it was young.

There's a loophole in the bank/checking system which can be exploited to reveal personal, some-times important information. If you have another person's checking account number (perhaps from a check they wrote you) most banks will allow you to call a computerized robot and inquire if the check is good. Well, during this call the robot asks you how much the check is written for... so, through multiple calls and trial/error you can determine how much money is in that person's account. Simply start high with a number such as $10,000. The robot will reply with "Sorry, there are insufficient funds to cover that check." Hang up, call back and enter "$5,000" and so on until you get a round-about idea of the actual balance. I've never done this, but I think it's been done to me!

Magnificently *huge* vegetables and fruit can be had right on your back deck or balcony with the stupendous invention called The Earth Box http://www.earthbox.com   It's a black box, about 12 x 24 inches which keeps the bottom of itself clear for watering. The ingenious aspect of it is the watering/nutrient system which is foolproof (you can't overwater it or dilute the soil.) Don't be tempted to add more seeds than recommended or you'll be forced to thin away perfectly good plants. I grew tomatoes first in mine and they were perfect beyond description. They made the produce section of my grocery store look like a third world market. Look at the pictures, follow the directions, you can't fail. (When I tried corn, I could see a difference in the plant grown every couple of hours!)
If you run a web site, be certain to use the tools

provided to check on your bandwidth use. If you have a lot of interesting material, other website owners will (rudely) link directly to your images and run up your bandwidth with their traffic. You never know when you've hit upon a truly interesting item that will be cross- linked all over the place, but *you'll* have to pay the bill for bandwidth. Check it often.

Humming can clear your stuffy nose or sinuses. Hum for a full minute or two every few hours, or as needed to vibrationally clear blocked nasal passages. This won't work with a cold because the tubes are clogged anyway and your sinuses will produce more muck immediately when you blow them out. But for simple everyday blockage, hum, or hold a hand-held massaging vibrator to your nose.

Pamphlet potpourri: our U.S. Gov't is a publishing fiend! The gov't printing house in Pueblo, Colorado has a fantastic online directory of it's zillion booklets -- order them on paper by just paying postage, or read the online version for free.

Every topic under the sun, and then some! http://www.pueblo.gsa.gov/

Unless you're an 80-year-old blue hair who enjoys

waiting in a 40 minute line at the post office to buy a single stamp to mail a Hallmark card to her college grandson who only cares if there's money in it, then avoid the post office like the plague and order your stamps online. Shipping is free! The also have many tools for calculating postage rates, overseas forms, etc. Just do it yourself. http://www.usps.gov

Don't put pasta or rice (specifically) down the kitchen drain through the disposal. The blades of the disposal will simply chop them into finer bits which will still stick to the pipes and clog them like an artery. Instead, just remember to scrape pasta and rice leftovers into Tupperware or the garbage.

Another thing we mostly disregard while in school is vocabulary. Increase it! Every day! The more words you know, the more your brain can exactly figure out how to express your thoughts and descriptions. You'll not only sound smarter to other people, you will, in fact, *be* smarter. As comedian Steve Martin said during his act, "Some people have a way with the English language, other people... well, uh, they 'no have way' I guess." A free and easy way is to subscribe to Wordsmith's wonderful Word-A-Day email newsletter. They'll send you a cool word, it's definition and an interesting usage in a sentence.

Well, that's all I have for now, but I'm starting a new collection of Middle-Aged Magic for my next book!

If you have a tip you'd like to share, PLEASE DO -- I welcome all e-mail ideas or questions to:

Uncle-Url@linkydinky.com

Linky & Dinky Enterprises
P.O. Box 418
Oldsmar, FL 34677

Linky & Dinky's
Secret Web Sites

(for legal reasons, we have to call these "Infotainment")

THERE MUST BE 2000 WAYS to use WD-40 SPRAY OIL
Scrub the pots and pans, Stan
   Clean piano keys, Lee
      Loosen stubborn nuts, Putz
         Just spray it as you please.
Wipe up candle soot, Toots
   Lubricate a lock, Jock
      Shine your bowling ball, ya'll
         Just spray it as you please.
http://www.twbc.org/wd40.htm

    * * *

**SEND YOUR MESSAGE IN A BOTTLE
ANYWHERE GLOBE-WIDE!**
Fill out the form, pick your exotic beach
location, and the kind folks who live there will
toss your message in a bottle out to sea. Amazing.
http://www.conwasa.demon.co.uk/miabix.htm

    * * *

LIFEHACKER
You can slip through life quicker and richer if
you know the MacGuyveresque tricks to living
in a modern society.
http://www.lifehacker.com/

YOU CAN BE A HUMAN LIE DETECTOR
Police detectives are EXPERTS at these
obvious (and not so obvious) body language
guffaws that scream "I'M LYING".
http://www.blifaloo.com/info/lies.php

* * *

100 WAYS TO CHEAT the MAN
Livin' Large on modern trickery and clever deceit.
http://www.cockeyed.com/magic/cheap/cheap.html

* * *

TINKER with your BAD HABIT SPREADSHEET
See how the combination of your unhealthy
indulgences reduces your lifespan, then fudge
the numbers to see if it's worth quitting
one or more of them. Makes you think!
http://www.nmfn.com/tnetwork/longevity_game_popup.html

* * *

TOP SECRET RECIPES (or, "Homemade Restaurant Food")
Expert chefs concoct easy-to-make duplicates
of famous restaurant and fast food culinary
delights. Who else will teach you to make Oreos?
http://www.topsecretrecipes.com/

BIG BROTHER NOT ONLY OBSERVES, he keeps stats
Everything about American life and business,
expressed as a percentage.
http://www.fedstats.gov/

* * *

BE A SPY ON THE INTERNET! (Snoop Public Records)
How much did your neighbor pay for his house?
What liens does your boss have against him?
How many robberies in your neighborhood?
It's endless, it's FREE, it's Public records!
They're public for a reason.
http://www.searchsystems.net/

* * *

THE WAY WaaaY BACK WWW ARCHIVE
What did web sites look like in 1996? Punch in
your favorites: LinkyDinky.com, Yahoo.com,
MSN.com, DrudgeReport.com, ARTBELL.COM, etc.
they're all there... in their infancy. Fascinating!
I can't believe what my hair looked like on our old web site!
http://www.archive.org/web/web.php

* * *

TEEN LINGO (a DictoGuide for old farts)
Thos crazy kids, it's as if they have a secret word
for everything!
http://www.thesource4ym.com/teenlingo/index.asp

VACATION FUN: Take a Factory Tour!

This nifty DB click-finds manufacturing assembly
plants the public can tour for free, all across
the country. Distilleries, toy factories, candy,
cheesemakers, glassblowers, etc. Take a detour,
see stuff being made. We've got it Made, in America
http://factorytoursusa.com/Index.asp

       *   *   *

NOBODY has "imchrismatthewsletsplayhardball.com" Yet!

DomainSurfer lets you see all the web sites which
contain a certain word in the domain name. Oddly,
the most common word used in domains is "sex".
http://www.domainsurfer.com/

       *   *   *

MOVIE CLIFF NOTES

The whole story, from beginning to end, in a
quick 5 minute read. You'll be able to lie
about seeing any movie quite convincingly.
http://www.themoviespoiler.com/

       *   *   *

3,000+ WORLDWIDE TV STATIONS airing on your PC

Surely with 3,000+ channels there's something good
to watch! Now we need a web-based TiVO for this.
http://wwitv.com/

MORE NEIGHBOR SNOOPING, money & politics

Punch in your zip code, see the NAMES
and ADDRESSES of your NEIGHBORS and
how MUCH MONEY they gave to political
candidates. Amazing.
http://www.fundrace.org/

*   *   *

THE PREDATOR NEXT DOOR!

Sex Offender Registries all 50 states.
Knowing where they are is just the beginning.
http://www.fbi.gov/hq/cid/cac/states.htm

*   *   *

GOOGLE NEWS ALERTS - INDISPENSABLE

I'm still using this since the very day
it came out! That alone is an accolade for greatness
on the internet.
http://www.google.com/alerts

*   *   *

RIP-OFF PRIMER

Learn the psychological tricks sleazy salesmen use
to make you buy when you don't want to.
http://www.trampolinesales.com/ripoffs.htm

You'll admit: EVERYTHING YOU BELIEVE IS WRONG!
This thing is incredible -- No matter how SURE or
DOGMATIC you are, and regardless of how deep your
religious beliefs about God, this deceptively
simple True/False quiz will logically twist your
convictions into a mobius strip of contradictions.
No wonder philosophers can't get chicks
http://www.philosophyquotes.net/cgi-bin/god_game1.cgi

*   *   *

TV ALERTS via EMAIL
TVeyes listens to 500 TV channels simultaneously
and sends you a text transcript when your keywords
are spoken on the air. Pretty cool!
http://consumer.tveyes.com/

*   *   *

TIME-TRAVELLING E-MAIL!
Yes! Send an e-mail to *yourself* into the future.
1 year, 2 years, 5 years, any distance, and that
e-mail will be held and sent back to you at the
indicated time. Make your message private or
public... Read other people's messages too!
(I just love elegant web ideas like this.)
http://www.futureme.org/

*   *   *

EVERY U.S. LAW ON THE BOOKS: The Federal Code
Is what you did last night a crime?
See if the 10 Commandments are in there
http://www4.law.cornell.edu/uscode/

ALL THE CHARITIES FIT TO HELP
Punch in your zip code and find the local
Orgs that need your help, your friendship,
but not necessarily your money. Lend a hand!
http://www.volunteermatch.org/

* * *

THE RULES FOR EVERY GAME EVER DEVISED
EveryRule has become the Authority on the rules and instructions for every game on the planet. Kid's Party Games, Casinos,
Card Games, Board Games, Drinking Games, Hi Ho Cherrio,
(even adult party games).
http://www.everyrule.com/

* * *

SECRET DVD FEATURES: THE HIDDEN MOTHERLODE
Those DVD movies you've been collecting are hiding secret
features, such as gag reels, featurettes, music videos and other
behind-the-scenes clips! I found a concealed 60-min. shag-
larious feature on my Austin Powers DVD! Here's how to
unlock all.
http://www.dvdeastereggs.com/

* * *

ROADSIDE AMERICA -- Offbeat Tourist Attractions
This is one of our favorite sites, and it's time
to run it again for the Summer Vacation Planning
Period -- click around the area you'll be
traveling to and see what kind of craziness the
locals have prepared to get your five bucks.
http://www.roadsideamerica.com/

CHEAP GAS
Now that Iraq has fallen, gasoline prices should be back to
25 cents a gallon, but until then, use the Gas Buddy
to find the cheapest fuel pumps in your city.
http://www.gasbuddy.com/

*   *   *

GOOGLE UNEARTHS PRIMORDIAL MUSINGS on USENET
They've discovered the 1st posts to things like MTV,
the Y2K bug, New Coke, AOL, the first post-WTC
messages, many more, all appearing like scratches and
drawings on ancient cave walls.
Some crazy web startup company called "Amazon" is hiring
http://www.google.com/googlegroups/archive_announce_20.html

*   *   *

MINOR FACTS ABOUT 967 MAJOR THINGS
Memorize all these, and you'll be able to add your 2 cents
to any party conversation. "Most of the lights in
the night sky are galaxies, not stars. We can only see
individual stars in our local galaxy. Wanna date me?
http://www.dustyinfo.com/

*   *   *

MISSING KID PREVENTION
Download Pres. Bush's new 12-page guide. It has some
great tips to protect your children, and what to do
immediately if your child is suddenly missing.
http://www.missingkids.com/

3000 ONLINE NEWSPAPERS WORLDWIDE
Find out that "Fair and Balanced" doesn't necessarily mean "accurate". And also if you're tired of the endless repeating of the "top news story". The cacophony of Free Speech is accessed through our keyboards, not the TV.
http://www.onlinenewspapers.com/

* * *

WHAT ARE PEOPLE SEARCHING THE NET FOR RIGHT-THIS-MINUTE?
Not so much Britney as we've been led to believe...
(hit RELOAD as often as you like for a new set)
http://www.metaspy.com

* * *

MURPHY HAS A LAW FOR EVERBODY
"If it's stupid, but it works, it isn't stupid."
"All bleeding stops. Eventually."
http://www.murphys-laws.com/

* * *

PHARMACEUTICAL DATABASE
Every prescribed drug. Elvis knew them all!
http://www.rxlist.com/

THE DOCTOR IS ONLINE
Tell the WebMD your symptoms, he'll
tell you what's wrong
http://www.webmd.com/

* * *

TRACK DOWN REGULAR PEOPLE WHO HAVE MOVED
Where'd they go? This might help you find out.
http://www.semaphorecorp.com/wdtg/wdtg.html

* * *

SNOOPING GEAR
Everything amateur and professional private eyes use.
http://www.spystuff.com/

* * *

THE BESTEST WEB SITE IN THE WORLD!
Linky & Dinky continue to bring hundreds of
thousands of fans weekly fun reports of
the most interesting, sometimes astonishingly
smart, clever, ridiculous and outrages web
sites the kooks on the internet can dream up.
Sign up quickly for Linky & Dinky's free
weekly email newsletter!
http://www.linkydinky.com

And of course, the motherlode...

Linky & Dinky's
Secret Clubhouse !
The largest,
most awesome and
jaw-dropping collection of
webmazement
your eyes will ever see.

Join us!

http://www.linkydinky.com/amazing.html

Mention Uncle Url's Book

(this one --- the one you're holding!)

Get **50% off** an
Annual Membership!
WOW!

http://www.linkydinky.com/amazing.html
.